SOFIA'S PROMISE

SOFIA
BOOK ONE

SYLVIANE STOLTZMAN

 Created with Vellum

For my sister and husband. Thank you for everything.

CHAPTER
ONE

A crash startled me as I drifted to sleep. I hopped out of bed and threw on my robe then grabbed my candle and lit it as fast as my shaky hands could. Holding the candle at an arm's length, I looked around for a sign of what had fallen. My room appeared just as I had left it when I'd gotten into bed. Nothing seemed out of place. I checked my water basin. The water wasn't moving. Maybe I had fallen asleep, and a dream had scared me awake.

My mind had been so overactive lately that Mother had told me I would never find a husband in my current state. I was barely fifteen, and Mother could hardly wait to get me out of the house. Her greatest desire in life was to marry me off to a wealthy family, as she had with my sister. Mother also searched for a bride with a nice dowry for my brother. So far, she had found it hard to locate a lady willing to move down the wealth ladder.

My door creaked as I eased it open, and I held my breath for a moment. I didn't want to wake anyone else in the household, but I wanted to find what had crashed before I could fall asleep. The wooden floor chilled my bare feet, and Mother would have a fit if she saw me without my slippers. She would insist cold feet could make me ill, just like her mother had always told her.

I completed my short trek down the hallway and didn't see anything out of the ordinary. Our all-gray cat, Oscar, streaked across the hall from my brother's room to my parents'. I glanced into my brother's room and saw his mop of black hair peeking out from under the comforter. His arm hung over the side of the bed. Odd. He never slept like that. I edged into his room to take a closer look. He grunted and pulled his arm under the blanket.

I shook my head and couldn't help but smile. "You aren't sleeping at all, you fake. You just saw my candlelight," I whispered.

A grin spread across his face. He sat up and cocked his head. "What are you doing up? You were supposed to be sleeping."

"Something startled me, which I now presume was you." I shook my head.

He had always been the rebellious one. Our sister was the well-behaved, proper one, and thankfully, she'd married into a great family.

"Go back to sleep. Nothing to concern yourself with," he said.

"Oliver, you can't keep sneaking out like this. Think of your reputation, as Mother would say. She'd just die if she knew. What were you off doing this time?" I asked.

"Sofia, don't worry about it." He grunted and flopped back, rolling over and wrapping himself in his blanket.

"But I need to worry about it. If you get caught, you know your bridal choices will get even slimmer than they already are."

"Who wants to marry a tailor's son? We're not wealthy enough."

I sat on the foot of his bed. I completely understood what he meant. He didn't realize how important he and Father were to our small community.

"You and Father are the best tailors around. Nobody's clothing looks nearly as nice as what you two create."

"The rich women aren't exactly lining up to marry me. You know Mother wants a woman with a dowry. I don't think that'll happen."

It suddenly made sense. "Ah, I see. You've fallen in love. I've seen how you two look at each other." I grinned because I had seen him flirting with different girls, but I had no idea who had struck his fancy.

"You see nothing. Go to bed. I need my rest." He covered his head with his blanket.

Defeated, I crept back to my room and resolved to pay closer attention to which girls he kept an eye on. I bet one of them would stand out if I watched closer. Oh, Mother would not like that.

As we sat at our dining table, eating breakfast, nobody spoke. I tried to remember my place, but sometimes, it was just so difficult. I often wondered if I would be anybody's wife, since I had a hard time keeping my thoughts to myself.

After nearly finishing breakfast, I could contain myself no longer. In the most ladylike whisper I could muster, I asked, "What's going on?"

Mother glared at me, as I expected her to since I spoke out of place. Her blue eyes turned to ice as her face reddened. Father, a quiet man, stroked his mustache but didn't look my way. My brother simmered, as he usually did when we all dined together.

Oliver looked at each of us. "No? No takers for Sofia's question?"

"Oliver, do not start," Mother warned, glancing sideways at Father.

"You don't want Sofia to know that you've completely upended our lives?"

"You're being dramatic. You really shouldn't be upset over so fine a match. She's quite wealthy," Mother said.

"So fine a match for you maybe." Oliver's voice rose, his knuckles turning white as he gripped his fork.

"Oliver, mind your mother." Father didn't raise his voice, but his tone held warning.

"Really, Father? I cannot believe you support this. You and Mother were pushed into marriage by your parents, and look at the headache that's caused all of us. We all must live with your unhappiness."

"Enough!" Father yelled.

Oliver and I jumped in our seats. Father never raised his voice at us. I glanced at Oliver, who sat with his mouth hanging open.

"I think I've had enough breakfast this morning. May I be excused?" he asked, shocking me with his politeness.

Father cleared his throat and looked at Oliver. "Go."

My brother wasted no time grabbing his plate and leaving the table.

"I don't know why you're always so easy on him. You know he's going to hurt our name," Mother scolded, poking at her food with her fork.

Father focused on his plate and continued eating without a word. Mother huffed and excused herself from the table. I felt sorry for Father. He wasn't angry or mean, and he and Mother clearly had no love between them, but he still protected her. He and I never seemed to fight, but I liked to believe that we understood each other the best.

"Would you like to have an outburst too?" Father asked, startling me out of my thoughts.

A giggle escaped my lips, and I covered my mouth.

"No need to be proper when it's just the two of us. Your mother can try to turn you into a lady all she wants, but I enjoy your soul." Father held his newspaper up in front of his face as I gaped at him.

I shook my head, clearing the shock from my system. I didn't bother excusing myself, as we all knew Father's newspaper was dismissal enough. Once he got into his news, he shut out the world around him.

I left the table to head outside. Mother didn't usually venture there when she was mad at my brother, so I could avoid her until she cooled off. When she was upset, she usually forced me to take lady lessons. I was not a fan. Hold my chin up, back straight, chest out. Don't cross my legs. Put my feet on the floor. I wasn't sure I was cut out to be a lady.

Grabbing my shawl just in case it was cool outside, I left through the back door. The brisk air woke me, but thankfully, it wasn't too cold. I hurried away from our small home toward the woods and my swing.

As I walked down the trail, a few branches stuck out. I had to maneuver around them so they didn't grab my shawl. My trail had become overgrown since I was the only one who walked it. Even Oliver didn't use the trail anymore. We used to go together as kids to swing or just have fun outside, but not so much as we got older. He was too busy flirting with whoever had caught his interest that week.

The trail stretched about half a mile down the small hill in our backyard. Something scurried through the leaves to my right, and I paused. Harmful wildlife was rare in our area. But I had heard the periodic story of a startled bear attacking out of self-defense, and I figured it was safest to stop and not move a muscle.

I waited and listened, but after a minute of no sound, I decided to continue. I reached my swing's clearing and stopped right at the end of the trail. Something had been here. Something quite large. The grass had all been trampled and resembled an enormous hen's nest. I held my breath and listened for sounds around me. Nothing.

Tiptoeing toward my swing, I kept my eyes on the ground. Besides the trampled grass, nothing else seemed out of the ordinary. I decided to walk around the edge of the clearing and found the place where the large whatever-it-was had left. The brush branches had been pushed apart and broken. Some of the leaves were stained brown. It was too early for the leaves to be changing, but when I leaned closer, I realized it was dried blood. I gasped and backed up a few steps, watching for the creature.

Still no sound. I couldn't help but follow the old blood trail. Whatever animal it belonged to should no longer be around. I pushed my way through some branches and avoided broken ones. Not more than fifty feet from the clearing, I heard labored breathing.

I removed my shoes and crept forward. Something shiny and black moved beyond the leaves. Its strained breath sounded like it was dying. I paused where I was because if the animal wanted to protect itself, it might not hesitate to kill me in its distress.

I moved a step closer and parted the leaves to get a better look. Right in front of me stood the first dragon I'd ever seen.

TWO

I couldn't help the gasp that escaped my lips as I fell backward. I scurried away from the dragon as fast as I could, tripping over my skirt.

"I will not hurt you," the creature said in a deep, gravelly voice.

I stopped and listened.

"Child, I will not hurt you," it said again.

There's no way a dragon could be talking to me, could there? All I'd ever heard about dragons was how rare and dangerous they were. Their only purpose was to destroy humans and livestock. Our village had never seen one, as far as I knew, but not many people were willing to discuss dragons with a young girl. Women were supposedly too fragile to handle such topics.

My curiosity got the better of me, and I crept forward to the edge of the leaves. "Do I have your word that you won't hurt me?" I had read somewhere that dragons always stayed true to their word.

The dragon sighed. "Yes, you have my word. I will not harm you in any way. I am dying, child."

I pushed my way through the bushes and beheld the glorious, huge creature in front of me. I swallowed my nervousness that the dragon could kill me in an instant and stepped forward. I was the same size as its front leg. Beautiful obsidian scales covered its entire body, including the spikes along its spine. It adjusted itself and moved its wings, which had a silk-like sheen. Its eyes, the color of fresh spring grass, remained focused on me.

"What do you call yourself, child?" the dragon rumbled.

Startled out of my awe, I took a nervous step backward. "Th-They call me Sofia."

The dragon grinned if that was possible. "Sofia, Daughter of Wisdom, I'm so glad it is you who found me today. I call myself Chumana."

"Are you injured, Chumana?" I edged closer, looking for a wound.

"You cannot help me, Sofia, though I sense you wish to try. It's not possible to save me. My wound is too deep, and I've been injured for too long. I was flying, looking for food, when a dragon hunter spotted me and speared me through my shoulder. I flew too long and lost too much blood, so death is now upon me. We do not know each other, but I know you have a good heart."

"How can you be so sure?" I asked.

"Your initial reaction to me, besides natural fear, was concern."

"Oh. Well, wouldn't that be everyone's initial reaction?"

The dragon rumbled like an earthquake, and I realized she must've been laughing.

"Oh, Sofia, you have so much to learn of the world yet."

I sighed. Not only did Mother think I was too young, so did Chumana.

The dragon said, "I mean no disrespect, Sofia. It's simply

that you are so kind, you do not know the ways of unkind people. Most people see a dragon and wish to kill it, not wonder if it's hurt. But your kind soul is the reason I must ask you for a favor." The dragon inhaled sharply and adjusted onto her side.

I knelt beside her and put my hand on her shoulder. Her cold scales surprised me. I had always imagined dragons with fire-hot scales. I refused to withdraw my hand, though, because Chumana should know that I wished to help her.

Chumana's eyes held my own as she pulled her tail out from under a wing. I broke our gaze to see what she was dragging toward me. It was beautiful with iridescent, changing colors and looked an awful lot like an overgrown egg.

"Is that an egg?" My chest tightened in panic. *What could I do with an egg? The more important question, what could I do with an egg once it hatched?*

Chumana did her dragon giggle-rumble again. "Yes. It's my egg. I was trying to find a new home to better protect it when I got injured. I need someone to protect it and raise it somewhere hunters won't look. Our numbers are dwindling due to dragon hunting. I don't want us to go extinct."

"But I know nothing of how to raise a dragon or make sure your baby hatches. What if I kill it before it's even born?" I started sweating, and I thought my heart would beat right out of my chest. I couldn't accept that responsibility. *What would Mother think?*

Oh, Mother. She would dispose of the egg as soon as she laid eyes on it. *Unless...* Unless she could lead a suitor to believe it was worth a lot of money and served as my dowry. But I would never give it away. *And what would happen once it hatched?* It was not like I could hide a dragon under the bed.

"Sofia, you know more than you think. There is knowledge about you, an education perhaps. But my time is running short. Please, promise you will take care of my child." Chumana's eyes searched mine.

I didn't want to make a promise I wasn't sure I could keep. But I knew she was right. Her time was short as her breaths became more labored. She adjusted herself multiple times as if she couldn't get comfortable. Her black scales paled into a dark gray.

"I promise, but please, tell me how to care for it," I begged. I didn't want her child to die under my care.

"It's easy. Keep her egg warm until she hatches. You can even put her egg right in the fire if you're afraid she's too cold. Her shell should always feel warm to a human's touch." She inhaled sharply and closed her eyes for a moment. "And don't worry if her shell is so hot it burns you. As long as her shell is at least warm, you'll be fine. She cannot get too hot, only too cold. When she hatches, she will be very hungry. Dragons are self-sufficient, so all you need to do is set her loose someplace with rats or mice. She will take care of herself. If you feel the need to feed her, she can eat raw meat but will prefer her meat a bit scorched. She will not have flame to protect herself until she is bigger, so you needn't worry about that." Chumana coughed and laid her head on the ground.

I rubbed her shoulder, hoping to comfort her. "Is that everything I need to know?"

Chumana half grinned. "For now. My child will know how to take care of herself after hatching. Just keep her away from hunters, and you'll be okay. Now, please, take my child into your arms." Chumana slid her egg along the ground until it was right next to me.

I picked it up, surprised that it was warm.

"That is the perfect temperature, which the shell can maintain for a while. But I'd put her on embers overnight to keep the shell warm."

"Okay. Chumana? I'm very sorry you were hurt, but I promise I will take care of your child the best that I can." I clung to her egg and gave her a small, encouraging smile.

"I know, Sofia. I know. Thank you. You will be a great dragoness." Chumana closed her eyes and sighed heavily as all the air left her body.

Tears fell down my cheeks. I couldn't believe she was gone. The magic of the moment was lost in her death. I sobbed as I sat in the grass and leaves, holding her child. I hadn't even thought to ask if other dragons would help me or where I could find them.

I reached out to touch Chumana one last time, but she disappeared. Her entire body burst into gray ash that slowly spiraled upward. I lay on my back as I watched her ashes ascend into the sky. Staying there, I stared until I couldn't see her any longer. Knowing that she was headed toward the heavens gave me a small comfort. Maybe that meant she would be watching over us. Me and her baby—her baby that I wasn't sure she had even named. I really wished that I had thought to ask her so many more questions.

After some time, I sat up and looked at the egg in my arms. It was still iridescent, and I was mesmerized by the colors. I had to figure out how to get it into the house and onto the hearth without anybody noticing. I wished myself luck and set off down the path toward home.

THREE

The egg was a lot heavier than I thought it should be. *But what do I know about dragons?* I needed to go and see what books I could dig up about dragons. My family's library was not large, but my sister's was. Her new, rich husband had his very own library, in fact. I wondered what sister dearest would think about her little sister coming to visit her. We'd hardly even heard from her since she'd married and moved away.

I was almost to the clearing behind our house when I heard Mother's frantic call, "Sofia! Where are you, girl?"

I hadn't been gone that long—I didn't think. *Who knows?* I always seemed to lose track of time. I really didn't want to leave Chumana's egg, but I knew my mother would lose her mind if I brought it to her after being out for so long. I searched my immediate area and found a perfect nest of bushes. I placed the egg inside and covered it with leaves. Nobody really came back there anyway, but I wanted to be careful. I stepped back and assessed my camouflage. The egg looked well concealed, so I dusted off my skirt and hurried toward Mother's voice.

"There you are, girl. You're a mess! What on earth have you been doing?" Mother gave me a typical disapproving glare.

"I'm sorry, Mother. I lost track of time." I bowed my head in obedience.

"You lose track of everything. Come in, and get cleaned up. You have a suitor here."

"I what?" I coughed.

"A suitor. And he's wealthy. So do your best and behave."

Mother grabbed me by the arm and hauled me inside. She took me the back way to avoid the suitor's eyes then shoved me into my room and closed the door behind us. I went straight to work on my hair, which I noticed had some leaves in it. *Whoops.* Then, as I finished working out the tangles, Mother brought me a fitting dress for a suitor. She took over my hair, brushing and pulling so hard I thought my neck might snap in two.

When I was presentable, which went remarkably fast, Mother said she would come back and get me in just a moment. I had nothing to do but stand in my bedroom. My frizzy black mess of hair was difficult to style, so she'd forbidden me to ever lie down once we did my hair. She didn't want anything interfering with how much work we had to put into taming my mane.

Mother opened my door and considered me from head to toe. "I guess this is as good as you'll get. Don't mess it up."

I lowered my head. "Yes, Mother."

Following her out into the parlor, I shook my head. Obedience and a proper life just weren't for me. I couldn't imagine the suitor would be any different from the others. So far, they had been snobbish, which my mother didn't care about as long as they were wealthy.

Mother cleared her throat as we entered the parlor. "Gabriel, I would like you to meet my daughter, Sofia. Sofia, this is Gabriel of the House of Thomas." Mother turned and threatened me with her eyes. It always amazed me how mothers could do that.

I plastered on my obedient-daughter smile and turned my attention to Gabriel. I was taken aback by how handsome he was. His thick brown hair was perfectly combed. His hazel eyes glinted with amusement, and his tight-lipped grin made him look like he was trying to suppress laughter. His black coat and cream trousers were immaculate. Even his boots didn't have a single speck of dust on them. I knew the Thomases were wealthy, but he looked pristine.

As I curtsied, I bowed my head and put on my shy-girl routine. "It's a pleasure to make your acquaintance, Mister Thomas. What brings you to our humble abode?" I purposely avoided looking at my mother, sure she didn't appreciate my obvious disdain for the surprise suitor call.

Gabriel's eyes narrowed as he assessed me. "They told me you were beautiful, but I didn't expect the rumors to be so true."

"I beg your pardon?" I snapped.

He laughed, and I immediately disliked him more than I had at hearing his last name. The Thomases were nothing but trouble. A bunch of spoiled rich people who never helped the poor, last time I checked.

"I'm sorry, Sofia. I just wanted to break the ice," Gabriel said.

Father guffawed, and I glared at him. Mother had her hand on her chest, obviously petrified that I would botch the whole meeting in the first minute.

"You're forgiven. I'm surprised you aren't as tart as most wealthy people." I sweetened my blow with the best apologetic smile I could muster.

"Sofia," Mother scolded.

"I beg your pardon, Mother. I must have had too much sun today." I inclined my head toward her, and her face was so red, I feared she might explode. I would definitely be in trouble later.

"Sofia, why don't you sit down? We can talk about things that you enjoy," Gabriel said.

I raised an eyebrow at him. No suitor had ever cared to ask what I enjoyed. We usually heard about their hunting trips or wealth. I debated for a moment then figured perhaps I would be less in trouble later if I played along. I walked to the love seat across from Gabriel and sat. When I did, he followed suit and took the chair behind him.

"So, Sofia, what do you enjoy doing in your free time?" Gabriel asked.

I knew it was a trick question. I couldn't win. Mother would expect me to say things like needlework and taking care of a household. Father would expect me to be honest. *Gabriel... who knows what he's thinking?* Maybe I could safely talk about books. It wasn't completely unheard of for women to read. Wealthy women could read and write.

"I enjoy reading."

"Oh? So do I. We have a wonderful library at my home that—"

"You have a library?" I startled myself and dropped my eyes to my lap. "I apologize. I did not mean to cut you off."

"No problem at all. Yes, we have a library. Perhaps you and your family would enjoy coming to see it? How would you all feel about coming to our home for an evening meal? We can reach out to you with a date." Gabriel turned to face Father. "Unless tonight would be okay?"

Father looked at Mother, whose mouth fell slightly ajar. Most suitors left in a huff after five minutes with me, not inviting us to dine.

Mother's look must have been enough because Father said, "We would love to dine together tonight. Let us know what time you would like us to arrive, and we will be there."

Gabriel and Father both stood and shook hands.

"Thank you, sir. I would say that seven should be a nice time. If it needs to be changed, I will let you know right away. I look forward to seeing you later." Gabriel turned to Mother and me. "Ladies, thank you for your company." Gabriel excused himself and went out the door.

I couldn't help but stand in shock. I already despised the wealthy, unwanted suitor. He seemed to find me amusing. *Who did he think he was?* I turned, and Mother stared at me with tears in her eyes.

"Mother?"

"Oh, darling. I think you just found yourself a match."

FOUR

Oh no. A match? I didn't want to be forced into a marriage. I still held on to the hope of finding someone on my own, even though I knew pretty much everyone in Holltree and the surrounding areas. Perhaps I would have to up my game to scare him away like I had the others that had shown up on our doorstep. Obedient, subservient wife was not exactly what I hoped for in my future, though it opposed Mother's hopes.

I hurried outside after Gabriel left. I didn't want to see Mother get all emotional about finally finding me a match. Father had been unreadable as usual. I never knew whether he wanted me to behave more ladylike or if he enjoyed my randomness. Mother had wailed when Celeste left, but she had always been her obvious favorite. She just hoped for the best for Oliver and me.

I didn't see anybody else outside, so I thought it best to grab Chumana's egg. I regretted that I still wore the dress Mother had made me wear, but oh well. I didn't want to waste time changing. I needed to hide the egg in the house, where it would be safe.

I followed my path to where I'd left the egg and was pleased to see that where I had covered it was completely undisturbed. I knelt and picked up the egg then dusted off my dress. Before leaving the trail, I checked to see if anybody had ventured outside.

Nobody in sight, I hurried to the house and took off my shoes at the door so nobody would hear me. I feared it would be too soon to put the egg in the embers, so I wanted to place it in my bedroom beneath my pillows. My bed had already been made, so it should be safe there.

I hurried down the hallway and entered my room. Closing my door, I stood with my back against it for a moment, grateful that Mother hadn't seen me. She must be getting ready. Though I was shocked that she hadn't come to get me ready first. I hoped she wouldn't make me wear my suffocating corset, but I was fairly certain she would.

I created a nest of sorts with my pillows. I hoped the down in my comforter would help keep the egg warm while I was at dinner. Down kept chicken eggs warm, so it should hopefully work for a dragon egg.

Moments after I had covered the egg with my decorative pillows, a knock came at my door.

"Come in!" I yelled. Not ladylike at all. *Oops.*

Mother opened the door and shook her head at me. "Ladies ought never to raise their voice. You must remember that if you're to be a perfect bride."

I bit my tongue. It was no use arguing with her, especially not with a wealthy suitor on the table. I had to suppress my giggle as I pictured him as a nice pig dinner with an apple stuffed in his mouth. That was what most suitors seemed to be to Mother—nothing more than an offering to make her part of another wealthy family.

Mother shuffled through my closet then pulled out a cobalt-blue dress. She held it out on her arm. "Yes, I think this dress will do nicely."

"Mother, our time to dine isn't for hours. May I dress later?"

"I need to work on your hair. We will dress you after."

"When do I get lunch?" I would be very irritable if I didn't get to eat until seven.

"You can have some bread once I get your hair manageable."

"Yes, Mother." That was going to be one of the longest days of my life.

I HAD to admit as I stared at myself in the mirror that Mother was a fine artist. I barely recognized myself. Not one hair was out of place, as she had probably placed one hundred pins in it to make sure it didn't move. She even had me shake my head to be sure it stayed put. Then she painted my face to look like a porcelain doll. The finished effect took a lot of work. I hoped I wouldn't have to do that every day if we made it to marriage.

I planned to play Mother's suitor game until I could figure out how to support myself. I knew other women had done it. One very successful woman in our village owned a bakery, all on her own too. She didn't need or even want a husband. Several people in the village considered her an odd one, but I thought she was lovely. She always gave me some little treat when I went there on our errands.

My dress clung to me, and I could hardly breathe in the corset. I tugged at my dress, trying to get some air into my lungs as I shifted my weight from foot to foot. I didn't dare sit down because I didn't want to wrinkle my dress. Our carriage ride would do that for me. I might as well not make it worse.

Finally, our carriage arrived, and Mother checked me over one final time. She smiled at me and, surprisingly, seemed satisfied with my appearance. Oliver had come home in time for Mother to cluck at him until he was presentable too. He glared at me for not being obnoxious enough to make Gabriel refuse to invite us. I just shrugged. Oliver and I had always tried to ward off potential matches.

We arrived at Thomas Manor a short ride later, as they did not live too many miles away. A young, tall, handsome man opened our carriage door and offered Mother his hand. She took it ever so gingerly and stepped out of the carriage, nodding a thanks to the footman. Father followed behind her. Then it was my turn. I declined the boy's hand and let myself out. Mother's irritation, written plainly on her face, told me I had made the wrong decision. Her glare practically burned a hole through my skin, and she shook her head at me. I gave her an apologetic shrug and turned back toward the carriage.

Oliver stood right behind me and offered me his arm. Grateful to have him with me, I took it and let him lead me to the doors. I looked up at the home in front of us and tripped on my own feet. Oliver righted me without letting me land face-first in the dust. Their home was enormous, standing three stories tall with windows spanning each story. I felt like an ant at the bottom of an oak tree. Columned archways stood in front of the entry doors at the top of a short staircase.

"You could fit ten of our homes in here," I whispered to Oliver.

"No wonder Mother seems so happy to be here. Hey, if you marry this guy, you could live on one side and he the other, and you'd never have to see him."

Oliver and I giggled, which earned us another glare from Mother over her shoulder. She slightly shook her head, and we knew we were on thin ice. As we walked in silence, I wondered if I should tell Oliver about Chumana and her egg. He was a game hunter, but I didn't know if he would want to kill it or not. I would have to drop some hints and see what he thought.

The double doors opened for us as we walked up the last of the stone steps and entered the archway. My jaw dropped at the sight of their foyer. Multiple chandeliers hung from the ceiling, lighting the entire area. Lit sconces lined the walls as well. The huge white room appeared to have been decorated in gold. Even the furniture had gold trimming. Huge, gilded mirrors hung on the opposite wall.

Oliver elbowed me, and I closed my mouth. No use being a codfish when I met rich people.

A beautiful woman with long, wavy brown hair approached us with her arms out, welcoming us. Her emerald-green dress sparkled like diamonds. "You must be the Taylors. How very lovely to meet you. Welcome to our home."

She grabbed her dress and curtsied so deeply, I was afraid she would fall over.

"You are very kind to host us this evening." Father kissed her extended hand once she stood and faced him.

"We are pleased to be here. Thank you for the invitation." Mother perfectly returned the woman's curtsy.

"My name is Elizabeth. You already know my son, Gabriel. And my husband, Benjamin, expects you in the smoking room, Mister Taylor. Our butler will show you the way." Elizabeth gestured toward a butler who stood by a wall, apparently waiting for Father.

Father followed the butler, and Mother and Elizabeth walked side by side to a sitting area, where they sat next to each other. Oliver and I looked at each other and shrugged. We sat down across from them and listened to them speak of things like the fabric of each other's dresses.

I was beginning to feel faint from starvation when a serving bell rang. I turned and saw one of their kitchen staff standing in a doorway.

"The appetizers are served," the man said.

"Ah, perfect. Thank you, Lewis. We'll be along shortly," Elizabeth said.

It took everything in my power not to roll my eyes. I wondered what it must be like to be waited on day and night. *Does it make everyone shallow and spoiled?* Though Elizabeth did thank Lewis, so that was kind of her.

Finally, we all rose and followed Elizabeth down a long hallway and off into a large dining area to the food. I could hardly wait. Mother had only let me have bread earlier, just as she had said, so I was famished. Oliver knew exactly where I wanted to go and led me in that direction, but Mother stopped us by clearing her throat.

Oh, right. Rule one million and one: a lady never approaches the food first. It was going to be a long night.

CHAPTER

FIVE

After Oliver had gathered a plate for himself, I was allowed to go. Mother still gave me the stink eye, but I was starving. And unless she wanted a hungry outburst, I had to get some food in my belly. As I loaded up my plate, someone laughed.

I turned, and Gabriel stood right behind me.

"Hungry, are we?" He chuckled.

"Famished."

"Well, I'm glad we have some good food for you, then." Gabriel picked up a plate and filled it, making my plate look like I'd barely gathered any food at all.

I couldn't help but laugh. "Who's famished now?"

"Certainly not me. This is to share," Gabriel said.

"Oh." I flushed and suddenly felt very stupid.

Gabriel laughed. "I'm just kidding. Do people not tease in your household?"

I cocked my head. "We do, but I'm used to you wealthy types being a bunch of sticks in the mud. You're all about being proper and boring with no unique personalities."

23

I brought my hand to my mouth. Mother would have murdered me if she'd heard that. I quickly looked for her, but she and Elizabeth were speaking at the far end of the table.

"Don't worry. She can't hear you. My mother is great at capturing people's focus. However, I'm pretty sure Oliver heard."

Oliver's face was completely red. He squeezed his lips together like he was trying to not spit out whatever he had just taken a bite of. He covered his mouth and looked everywhere but at me. I glared at him, but that only seemed to make him worse.

"You're unusual, Sofia." Gabriel's eyebrows drew together, and his eyes searched my face.

"Unusual. That's a nice thing to say." I walked around him to sit across from Oliver.

Gabriel followed me to the table and sat by Oliver. "Unusual is not a bad thing. You know how you said rich people are proper and boring? Well, the ladies are the epitome of that. They offer zero good conversation."

"Good conversation, huh? What do you know about dragons?" I asked.

Oliver scoffed at me and scrunched his face, annoyed. Mother would have fainted. Gabriel, however, remained unfazed. I would really have to work harder to scare him away.

"Dragons? Why do you ask?" Not a hint of mockery tinged Gabriel's tone or posture.

"I've always been fascinated with mythical creatures. I'm just curious about your take on dragons. Do you think they're real or mythical, for starters?" I ate some of the fruit on my plate so Gabriel would have to talk for a while.

Gabriel rocked his head from side to side. Seeing as I'd never gotten so far with my suitors before, I wondered if they talked about anything out of the ordinary like dragons.

"I think that they are both mythical and real. Just because I've never seen one doesn't mean they don't exist. And I know others have seen them. But the mythical part is because we don't know much of anything about them. It's hard to know what is real and what is myth."

Hm. He was good.

"I could take you to our library and see what books we can dig up on dragons," Gabriel said.

I tried to hide my excitement, but it must have reached my face before I could turn it off because Gabriel half grinned at me.

"That would be lovely of you." I tried to contain the eagerness in my voice.

"How about after we eat this stuffy meal, us three can go see what we dig up?" Gabriel asked.

"Works for me," Oliver said to Gabriel, but he looked at me. I could sense suspicion in him. My brother knew me too well.

Just then, the dinner bell rang, and we moved down the table toward the adults. Mother motioned for me to sit across from Gabriel, next to her. She really did want that marriage to be the one. Oliver sat next to Gabriel, and our fathers sat near the table's end.

"How old are you, Gabriel?" I asked.

I sucked in air through my teeth as my mother pinched my thigh under the table. I tried to smile politely afterward, but I could feel the bruise blossoming beneath my dress.

Gabriel laughed but stopped when he saw Elizabeth staring at him. She looked just as unimpressed as my mother, tight-lipped and scowling.

"I'm eighteen. Why do you ask?" Gabriel used a perfect gentleman's tone and even added a polite smile.

He was making me work to drive him away.

"I was just curious about our age difference," I said.

"Well, what's your age?" Gabriel asked.

"Gabriel! You do not ask women such things." Elizabeth pursed her lips and shook her head.

"My apologies, Mother." Gabriel inclined his head toward her.

"So, how goes the tailoring business?" Mr. Thomas asked.

My father, startled, shook his head quickly and smiled. "It's going well. We have many reliable and returning customers to attend to."

"That's great news," Mr. Thomas said.

And so the conversation went over the duration of the meal. I could hardly contain myself, wanting to go to the library. Gabriel seemed to notice because he kept half laughing at me every now and then while our mothers glared at us. However, our fathers both seemed to find humor in the situation and repeatedly cleared their throats and changed the conversation between them.

At long last, the meal came to an end, and we children could be excused. The men retired to the smoking room to talk business while the ladies spoke about fashion. We were released to go to the library. Finally.

We walked through a few different hallways and up one story toward our destination. Their manor was shaped like a U, and the library was all the way at the end of the house. Gabriel led Oliver and me, explaining different rooms and paintings as we went. I really didn't care and was solely focused on dragons, but I had to play along until he got me to the library. I hoped my egg was doing okay under its blanket. I would have to wait until everyone was asleep before I could hide it in the leftover embers of the fireplace.

"Lost in thought?"

"Hm?" I turned to Gabriel.

"I asked you a question, and you didn't even respond. I know you dislike me, but I didn't realize it was that much."

"Oh, I'm sorry, truly. My mind was elsewhere."

"You didn't deny that you don't like me," Gabriel said.

Oliver laughed. "She doesn't like anyone."

"Oliver. You know that's not true. I like you for some inexplicable reason."

"You have to like me. I'm your brother."

"I don't have to like anyone." I quieted because it was odd to say such things in front of someone I'd just met without getting scolded by Mother.

"You two seem like you could be a lot of fun to spend time with," Gabriel said.

"Only if you want to play referee. We are constantly at each other's throats," Oliver said.

"I wouldn't know. I'm an only child," Gabriel said.

"Oh, that must be so lonely. I'm sorry," I said.

"Showing me kindness too? You really do want to get to this library. We had better get a move on. I'm surprised you haven't passed me up, since I told you where it was," Gabriel said.

"My mother taught me to behave like a lady," I said, then we all burst out laughing.

"Lady, my foot," Oliver said.

Gabriel just continued to laugh. Maybe he wasn't so bad. But I definitely didn't want to marry him. His mother was just like mine, and I couldn't forget that he was a wealthy brat. I cleared my throat. That seemed to quiet us all, and we didn't speak as we reached the library doors.

Gabriel stepped forward and pushed open the double doors that were as tall as the vaulted ceiling. I had to tilt back my head to see the tops.

"Welcome to our library." Gabriel waved his hand for us to walk in.

I gasped and clutched my hands to my chest. More books filled the space than I had ever seen in one place, including Celeste's new home. Every book ever written had to be in that library. I gaped, stepped forward, and spun a full circle. Books reached from floor to ceiling, and the ceilings had to be twenty feet high. Multiple ladders stood around the room with wheels to roll along the front of the bookshelves. Stairs wrapped around the edges of the room near the door with a walkway that led all around the second story.

"I've never seen so many books in my life. This is incredible. Thank you for bringing us here," I said.

"Just wait until you see all the topics we have. We even have books in other languages," Gabriel said.

"What good is that? I can only speak English," I said.

"Well, I can speak a few languages, so it does me some good. When you learn other languages, it will do you some good too," Gabriel said.

I glared at him. Of course he could speak multiple languages. His parents had enough money to afford the best education. I'd barely made it through school. Mother had only recently learned to read and write.

"I meant no disrespect." Gabriel's eyes never left mine.

"Yeah, Sof, he didn't mean to disrespect us poor people." Oliver elbowed me. "He just forgets that what's normal for him isn't normal for everybody."

"I truly apologize." Gabriel looked between Oliver and me.

"Apology accepted. You couldn't help what you were born into any more than I could." I looked around the room again. "So, if I were a book on dragons, where would I be?"

Gabriel grinned. "Well, you're in luck because we have a whole section on dragons. Follow me."

We followed Gabriel across the room, and he wasn't kidding about a dragon section. There had to be at least fifty books in it.

"You two have fun looking at dragon books. I'm going to wander the shelves if that's okay, Gabriel."

"Please, be my guest." Gabriel waved his arm in the direction of all the books.

I read the spines to see where I should even start. I highly doubted I would find a book on dragon raising. I ran my finger along the spines and was surprised that some felt like Chumana had. I jerked my hand back and looked at Gabriel.

"What are these covers made of?" I asked, suddenly sick to my stomach.

"I believe they're made of dragon skin." Gabriel ran his hand along one's spine. "I can't even imagine what that would be like... meeting a dragon. It must be the most amazing thing in the world."

My mouth went dry, and I couldn't seem to form words, but then I remembered how Chumana had turned to ash when she'd died. *What must they have done to the dragon to get hide for these books?* I felt queasy.

"I need to sit down a moment." I looked around for a place to sit.

Gabriel took my arm and helped me to the nearest chair.

"Lean over, and put your head down. It helps," Gabriel said.

I saw more feet beneath my face as I leaned over.

"What happened?" Oliver asked.

"I don't know. She was looking at the books then didn't feel well. Was it something you ate?" Gabriel asked.

I nodded. "It must've been. I'll be okay. Just give me a moment." I slowly breathed in and out through my mouth, slowing my heartbeat. I finally began to feel normal, and I eased myself back up. "I'm sorry. I don't know what came over me."

"You don't look so good, Sof. I think maybe we should head home," Oliver said.

No way would I leave without at least one book, so I shook my head. "I'll be all right. I just had a moment is all."

"Women can be fragile," Oliver said, looking at Gabriel.

Gabriel wisely didn't say anything in return.

Once the queasiness passed, I stood and walked back to the dragon section. I could feel both Gabriel and Oliver watching me. *Great.* I did not want them to think of me as a weak woman. Deterring Gabriel had proven hard enough. It would be harder if I couldn't keep up with his jests.

Again, I read through the different titles. There had to be something about young dragons, even if the book only hypothesized. I finally settled on one titled *Last of Their Kind*. It seemed promising when I flipped open the pages and saw information hinting at the young all the way to the old.

I looked up at Gabriel, and he said, "You can borrow that. We rarely read the books in here right now. It's more of a winter thing."

My smile must have reached my ears because Gabriel's did the same. Just as I was about to thank him, a butler entered.

"Your parents are waiting for you at the doors. It is time to head home," he said.

"Thank you, sir. We will be right along," Oliver said.

I turned to Gabriel and clutched the book to my chest. "Thank you for this. I really appreciate it."

"You're welcome." He grinned at me again.

Maybe he wasn't so bad after all.

CHAPTER

SIX

Mother glared at me with tight lips when I arrived at the doors with a book in my hands, but she waited to say anything until we reached the carriage.

"Ladies do not need to read all the time. It's simply not done," Mother said.

"But, Mother, don't forget that she borrowed one of Gabriel's books. That means he either must come retrieve it or she must bring it back, so they are guaranteed a second meeting," Oliver said.

I fumed silently at him because he was right, but I was also thankful that he knew how to get Mother off my case.

She considered that for a moment. "You have a point, Oliver. It would be nice to see Elizabeth again. She talked about their latest dinner parties and events going on around Holltree. It was fun having another woman to speak with, and she even invited me to attend a few gatherings with her."

Mother kept trying to turn me into a lady and wanted me to show an interest in becoming the best lady I could be, but I

31

kept saying and doing the wrong things. I just didn't share the same interests that she did. I would much rather be outside and barefoot than inside, struggling to breathe with a corset, talking to people.

The rest of the carriage ride home was quiet. Father didn't say a word the entire trip, though I thought he had enjoyed Mr. Thomas. Father was a man of few words, and it was often hard to tell if he preferred anybody's company.

I could hardly wait to get home and put Chumana's egg in the hearth. I didn't want to fail her on my first day. I squeezed the book tightly to my chest. Hopefully, something would tell me how to raise a dragon. But the worst question I had was where I could raise the dragon. I couldn't keep it in my room without someone noticing.

Those thoughts filled my brain for the entire ride home. I kept my attention on the window, feeling overwhelmed with my near future. I could feel my mother's glares, my father's concern, and my brother's nosiness boring into the back of my head.

Finally, our carriage stopped. Father thanked the driver as we headed into our house. It was late enough that we could probably get away with going straight to our rooms and not be suspicious, so I fake yawned.

"I'm going to bed. I'll see you all in the morning," I said.

Father extended his arm, and I curled in for a hug.

He kissed the top of my head. "Good night, Sof."

"Good night, Father."

Father half smiled at me, and I looked at Mother to see if she expected a hug or anything. When she turned away from me, I went to my room. Oliver had already shut his door behind him.

I tried to not be obvious about hurrying to my bedroom and closing the door behind me. Then, rushing to my bed, I pulled back the blanket and touched the egg. It still felt warm. A good sign. I just had to wait for my family to go to sleep so I could put the egg in the hearth. Then, I had to be up early enough to retrieve it before anybody stoked the fire. I changed into my nightdress, sat with the egg in my lap, and listened to my family's nightly routines. Soon enough, it would be time.

When I heard Father's soft rumblings, I knew everyone would be asleep. Grabbing a blanket, I wrapped the egg. If anybody happened to get up, I could claim I was sleepwalking with my blanket. Having the egg visible would be much more difficult to explain.

Holding my candle in one hand, I cradled the egg in my other arm. I crept to my door and eased it open. Peeking toward my parents' and brother's rooms, I checked for evidence of light under their doors or any sounds. I held my breath. Once satisfied that there was nothing to hear, I left my room and pulled the door slightly closed behind me.

I hurried down the hall and set my candle next to the hearth, debating how I would put the egg in the fire. I could move the wood aside and set it right in the middle, or I could put it toward the back of the hearth, where the heat was warmest. I sat cross-legged and considered my options. The heat would probably be best since it would only be for a few hours.

"What are you doing?"

I jumped and about fell into the fire. Flipping my blanket over the egg, I turned around. *Oliver.*

"What are *you* doing?" I whispered as I adjusted my body to block my blanket.

"I asked you first," Oliver murmured.

"I was chilly. I needed to warm myself."

"By sitting on the cold floor? Makes sense to me." Oliver smirked. He always knew when I was lying.

"You have your secrets, and I have mine. Go to bed." I refused to move and expose my egg-shaped blanket, which would arouse his suspicion even more.

"You know my secrets. Just not who with. I know nothing of yours," he whispered.

I sighed. *How much could I tell him? Would he think me crazy? Would he go straight to Father? Or even worse, Mother? Would he try to kill the dragon before it hatched?*

"Does this have anything to do with your dragon research?"

I tried to make my face blank, but as soon as I saw his grin, I knew I had failed. I didn't know why I even bothered trying to keep things from him. He knew me entirely too well.

He rushed to my side and dropped down next to me. "Is it a dragon?"

His bright, excited eyes and wide smile completely melted my resolve to do it alone. I sensed no malicious intent, so I hoped for the best.

"Don't laugh at me. And please, I beg you, don't tell Mother and Father." I searched his face for any trouble he might cause but saw nothing.

"I swear, your secret is mine. I will not tell a soul unless you approve of it." Oliver held up his hand as if swearing an oath.

"Good. No. It's not a dragon... yet." I turned and pulled the blanket off the egg.

Oliver gasped. "It's beautiful. How do you know it's going to be a dragon?"

"Well, I met its mother today, and she entrusted her egg to me. Someone had speared her, and she was dying. She needed to know that her baby would be safe, so I promised her I'd do my best. Though I honestly have no idea what I'm doing, and I wish I'd asked her more about how to raise a dragon before she passed. I wish I knew where more dragons were so I could give them the egg, but its mother, Chumana, never mentioned giving it to other dragons."

"You spoke to a dragon?" Oliver's eyes widened.

"She was beautiful, Oliver. But before we continue speaking of her, I really need to keep this egg warm. I think overnight would be fine in the hearth. So far, I've kept it just in my down blanket before now."

"Well, let's get it in the hearth. And we should cover it, just in case we aren't up early enough before someone stokes the fire. Wait. Will the fire hurt it?"

"No, silly. Dragons are fire. Well, I think they are. I have no idea. Will you help me get more books and study dragons? I want this one to live. I don't even know how long eggs incubate. I really should've asked Chumana more. I feel so dumb that I didn't."

"Sofia... the fact that you even spoke to a dragon is beyond amazing. Don't feel dumb. I don't know if I would've been able to speak, let alone carry on a conversation and agree to raise a baby dragon to save their species." Oliver grinned and nudged me with his elbow.

I couldn't help but smile back at him. For as big of a pest as he could be, I really did love him. We both took the opportunity to grab the shovel for ashes and made a hole for the egg. We then covered the egg until it would look like an odd mound of ashes to anybody else.

"I want to remove the egg early in the morning before anybody decides to load more wood in the fire," I said.

"I'll be sure to check on it if I'm up before you. Perhaps tomorrow, we can go back to your betrothed's house and see if we can do some more dragon research."

I pushed him. "That's not funny. He is not my betrothed. He is nothing more than a spoiled rich brat that I will scare away just like the others."

"Mm-hmm. Didn't seem that way to me, but what do I know? Not as much as you and Mother, obviously."

"Oliver, let's get to sleep. Please don't forget to check on my egg if you're up before me. And hide it in your blankets if you grab it." I stood and picked up my blanket, taking one last look at the egg under the ashes.

"I think you mean *our* egg, and of course I will. I wouldn't want Mother to see it. She'd probably try to use it for your dowry."

I rolled my eyes, but he was right. Mother would think it was worth a lot of money. Best to keep her away from it. We went back to our rooms, and I collapsed onto my bed, piling on my covers to stay warm.

I STRETCHED as sunlight warmed my face, and I sat up straight in bed. *The egg.* Grabbing my robe, I threw it on along with my slippers. I rushed to the hearth and stopped short. The lump of ashes was no longer there. Oliver must have taken it out already. I turned and hurried to his room.

Pushing open his door, I peeked inside and saw his shape under his mound of blankets. I rushed over and pulled back his covers.

"Hey! It's cold. Leave me be," Oliver grumbled, grasping for his blankets.

"Where is it?"

"Right here." Oliver rolled over and moved the other side of his comforter.

Sure enough, there was the egg, just as he had promised. I quickly put my hand on it to see how warm it was. It was almost too hot to touch.

"How is it so warm?"

"I have no idea. But when I woke up to check on it, it was too hot to carry. I had to put it in my blanket to bring it back to the room without burning myself. Now, let me sleep. It'll be safe in here."

"I'd feel better with it in my room." I crossed my arms and tapped my foot.

"Well, too bad. You and I both know Mother always creeps about your room. She never bothers to come into mine." Oliver closed his eyes, grinned, and cocooned himself inside his blankets.

I huffed. He had a point, though. Mother did enjoy snooping in my room. She removed anything that hinted at me not being ladylike. I knew she got nosy whenever I went outside. Several of my things had been misplaced before.

"Fine. But don't let Chumana down. She's counting on us."

Oliver peeked his eyes over his blanket and drew his eyebrows together. "I would never let her down. We'll figure out how to raise this dragon together."

"Okay. I'm going to go get some rest. Then my research truly begins."

I went back to my room, closed my shutters, and crawled under the covers to see if I could get a little more sleep.

CHAPTER

SEVEN

Still hiding underneath my blanket, I heard Mother fussing about my bedroom, mumbling to herself.

"Ladies should not have such messy rooms and sleep in so late."

I groaned as my blankets were ripped away from me, exposing me to the chilly air.

"Mother, what is the meaning of this?" I hurried to cover myself with my robe and put on my slippers.

"We received a message summoning you and your brother to the Thomases'." Mother's eyes sparkled.

"Did you get Oliver up yet?" I asked, fearing Mother might see the egg.

"He's already eating breakfast. You need to get ready now. Don't want to disappoint the Thomases. Oh, can you imagine having the Thomases for in-laws?" Mother clasped her hands in front of her heart and pulled her shoulders to her ears. She then returned to tidying my room.

I rolled my eyes and got myself ready. I then walked to the kitchen to see Oliver finishing his breakfast.

"You're up early." I scowled at him.

"Didn't want to miss an opportunity to make you uncomfortable around Gabriel." He winked.

"You're disgusting. And good luck with that. I cannot be made uncomfortable." I tried to glare at him but grinned instead.

"Challenge accepted."

I scoffed and got myself some breakfast.

Mother scurried out of my room with a couple of my older cloaks.

"What are you doing with my cloaks?"

"These are just rags now. I'm going to see if they can be salvaged for anything else."

"Mother, I like those cloaks." I wished she would stay out of my things.

"I don't care. We don't want to look like paupers with you out and about. What if Gabriel asks you to go for a walk and you grab one of these accidentally? That would be humiliating." Mother walked away.

I didn't bother to say anything. Once she got her mind set on something, I couldn't reason with her. She listened to nothing and no one. I would go later and steal them back, like I'd done with most of the things she'd removed from my belongings.

I felt someone looking at me and knew Oliver was trying to hide his laughter. I risked a glance at him, and we both burst out laughing.

"Quit reading my thoughts," I said.

"I can't help it. They're so amusing."

Oliver and I laughed until Mother came back into the dining area, glaring at us.

"Sorry, Mother," we said at the same time, lowering our heads.

Someone knocked at the door. Oliver and I shared a look. People rarely visited us.

"Sofia, be a dear and go see who is at the door, please," Mother said.

I sighed and went to the entry. Plastering on a smile that would please Mother, I opened the door.

"Good morning, Miss Taylor," Gabriel said as he dipped into a bow.

My smile dropped into a confused, contorted expression. "What are you doing here?"

"Sofia!" Mother shrieked from somewhere in the house.

"I-I'm sorry. What brings you our way? I thought we were supposed to go see you at your home?"

Gabriel's eyes sparkled. "I thought I'd come fetch you. No use making you come that way by yourself."

"I thought Oliver was to come too?" I asked, thoroughly confused.

"Of course Oliver is supposed to come too. I meant by your-selves." Gabriel's face flushed.

"Invite him in," Mother hissed.

I sighed and pulled the door open. "Please, come in."

Gabriel nodded a polite thanks and entered, sure to wipe his feet on our mat. "What a lovely home you have."

"No need to lie. Our house isn't even the size of your entry-way," I said.

"Sofia!"

Whoops. My poor mother was going to have a heart attack before our encounter had finished. Hopefully, we could leave soon.

"It isn't the size of the home but the feeling of home that matters," Gabriel said.

Mother rushed in, probably trying to save the day, and

curtsied. "Welcome to our humble abode, Gabriel. We are pleased to have you here."

"Thank you, Mrs. Taylor. Your kindness is appreciated," Gabriel said.

"Would you like something to eat or drink?" Mother asked.

"No, thank you. I just had breakfast before I came over. I hoped to get Oliver and Miss Sofia to come back to my house. We weren't able to finish our discussions, and I'd like to get to know them both better," Gabriel said.

It was interesting just how well he knew how to play my mother's personality. Delight painted her features. If she were a puppy, she would have been bouncing from paw to paw with her tail wagging so hard her butt shook. I grinned at the thought and looked at the floor.

"Oh, that's lovely. Let me go get Oliver. He should be right along." Mother left.

Gabriel turned his attention to me. "Did you want to bring that book with you? Maybe we could find something interesting in it."

I shrugged. "Yeah, I can go get it. But I can't leave you here by yourself. Mother would kill me. I'll go grab it when she brings Oliver."

"What are you hoping to find?" Gabriel's tone seemed curious, but I wouldn't reveal anything to him just yet.

"Well, I recently heard hunters talking about shooting down a dragon around here, and it piqued my curiosity. What if we had dragons nearby? What would they do to us? Or us to them?" That was mostly true. The thoughts had crossed my mind.

"I'll accept that answer. For now—"

"Accept what answer?" My mother's high-pitched squeal indicated she thought a romance was blossoming.

Oliver followed right behind her, smirking at me.

"That she enjoys my company," Gabriel said, "and would like to go on a walk with me sometime soon. I accepted the answer, even though she did not specify a time or date."

I could've hugged him. He must know how to keep a mother happy from experience with his own.

"That sounds lovely. Now, you all have a good time." Mother practically bounced with each step as she left. Yes, just like a puppy.

"I'll be right back," I said to Oliver.

I ran to grab the book and returned. "Is everything okay, Oliver? Before we go?"

"Yes, Sof. Everything's just fine."

I nodded. He knew I meant the egg, and we left the house for Gabriel's carriage.

The ride was completely uneventful. Gabriel and Oliver discussed normal things that I guessed boys learned to discuss to be men. Gabriel attempted to include me in the conversation, but I had opened my dragon book and was lost in thought almost every time he said my name.

"You know, Sofia, I don't know any other ladies who like to read about dragons. Especially nonfiction," Gabriel said.

My face flushed. Mother would've lost her mind if she'd heard him say that. She was always after me to be a lady, and a potential suitor had more or less just validated that I wasn't a lady, as Mother always said.

"Well, I guess I'm not much of a lady, then." I kept my voice pleasant.

"Just because other ladies don't do it doesn't make it wrong," Gabriel said.

My heart fluttered, and I looked at Oliver to see if he'd heard what I had. Deterring Gabriel as my suitor once I was done using his library would be tricky. It was hard to know whether he could see through my fake self or if he played the same game.

"Well, you don't seem like the typical snobbish gentlemen who have called on me before."

Gabriel mock gasped and clutched his chest. "You think I'm trying to call on you? Oh, no, Sofia. I heard that Oliver was an excellent card player, and I wanted to see if the rumors were true. I just had to tell my mother I was courting you to see for myself."

Gabriel's lips tightened as he tried to suppress his laughter, then all three of us guffawed.

"Gabriel, I may not be like the ladies you're used to, but I'm not kidding when I say that you truly aren't like the gentlemen I'm used to," I said.

"Yeah, Gabriel, you really are different. And we mean that in a nice way. Even our sister's husband is a bit of a snob with us being his poor in-laws," Oliver said.

"Oliver," I scolded.

Though I was no lady, even I knew it was completely improper to speak of how poor we were. Tailors didn't make much money. Sure, Father had plenty of clients, but the time it took to make everything cost us income.

"You know, I'd really appreciate it if you both stopped calling me Gabriel. I always feel like I'm in trouble. Call me Gabe, please."

I grinned. He was just as excellent as my brother at reading people and what needed to be said or done to lessen embarrassment.

"Gabe it is," I said, and Oliver nodded.

The carriage stopped, and Oliver and Gabe got out first. Gabe offered me his hand. I debated ignoring it, but I really needed to continue to play nice until my research was done. I placed my hand on his and allowed him to help me down the narrow step.

"My lady." Gabe inclined his head.

I smiled but chose not to return a comment. That wasn't too rude for a lady—at least I didn't think it was. He offered me his arm, and I reluctantly took it as we walked to his mini castle. I still couldn't believe how large it was. His butler swung the doors open for us as we approached.

We all walked up the staircase in a row of three. It was convenient that Oliver and Gabe enjoyed each other's company. That way, a lot of the conversation could be done between them while I could think about everything Chumana had told me, which wasn't much to go on. I knew, once the baby hatched, my true issues would begin. I had never been allowed to have a dog, let alone a dragon. Mother would lose her mind. I was curious how Father would respond. He was more forgiving, but a dragon could be our family's doom. I was grateful that our sister had already been married off, in case I ruined our family.

"You're doing it again," Gabe said.

I startled. "Excuse me?"

"You're in your little dreamland. Where do you go when you're there?" Gabe asked.

"Someplace nobody else can follow. Until I'm interrupted." I grinned.

Gabe smiled back and shook his head. Oliver made a kissy face, and I glared at him. That was not flirting. I would not give in to the spoiled, rich boy. I just needed his books.

We reached the library, and I spotted tea and three cups.

"I told the staff that we would need some refreshments while working in here," Gabe said.

I inclined my head and let go of Gabe's arm, since we were in the library, then went straight to the dragon section. I really didn't know what to look for. The book I held told me some information but not even close to everything I would need to know.

Oliver and Gabe stood on either side of me, looking at the titles.

"What about this one? It looks like it's a history of drag-ons," Oliver said.

I glanced over. "I think that would be a great start. See what you can find."

"I feel like I'd be more helpful if I knew what we were looking for," Gabe said.

Oliver shrugged one shoulder behind Gabe. *Thanks a lot.*

"Well, what we are looking for would be how dragons survived. Like if they were on their own," I said.

"I thought all dragons were on their own." Gabe's face seemed sincere.

"Well, all dragons have mothers. What would they do if something happened to that mother? Just think about how all the dragons are being hunted now. What if a baby dragon's mother and father were killed and it didn't know where to go to be taken care of or how to find family."

Gabe nodded the whole time I talked and continued looking at the dragon books. "So, maybe this one?" He handed me a book.

I read the title, *Are They Truly Vanishing?* "Yes, I think this would be good. Let's see what we can learn about dragons today."

NOTHING. That was what we learned about dragons. Gabe, Oliver, and I spent an entire day in that library, only stopping for lunch. We opened numerous books. None more helpful than the last. I felt utterly defeated. I let out an exasperated sigh and dropped my head onto the book in front of me.

"Perhaps we should take tomorrow off from our research," Gabe said.

I wasn't sure if I wanted that or not. I was frustrated with not finding anything about dragons that would help Chumana's baby. *But can I quit the search?* Or maybe one day off was what I needed to refresh my mind and find new, hopefully helpful information.

"Wait!"

Gabe and I jumped. Oliver leaped from his chair and kneeled beside mine.

Oliver read out loud, "'In rare instances, rare meaning it happens once every millennium at most, a dragon may entrust her offspring to the most loyal and trustworthy soul she meets at her life's end. Dragons have a sense about these things, better than any other living being. This chosen person, usually female, will become the living parent to their offspring until it is old enough to live on its own, which takes approximately twelve months. However, that chosen person will be an honorary dragon family member and will be accepted by most dragons. Not all dragons trust this system and may not accept the chosen person. If a mother should entrust her baby to another, that person should prepare for a tumultuous life, as they will not belong with dragons nor be accepted by humans.'" Oliver's eyes glistened as he looked at me. "Sof, are you okay?"

Tears filled my eyes. This couldn't be happening. I should never have agreed to help Chumana and her baby. But she chose me. I was her chosen soul. *Did she know she'd find me there? Was it entirely by chance?* One year until the dragon could fend for itself. *What am I to do with a dragon for a year?* I had nowhere to stash a full-grown dragon. A baby, sure, I had ideas, but a full year would be impossible. If one sheep went missing, the dragon would be blamed.

"I know something's going on, and I'd really appreciate not being completely in the dark," Gabe said.

I gulped and wiped my eyes. "My apologies, Gabe."

"That's it? No explanation?" Gabe asked.

"I think it's time we go home. I'm—I'm not feeling very well," I said.

Gabe scoffed. "Fine. If you ever deem me worthy to know what you two are up to, you know where to find me." He clenched his jaw, turned, and left us alone in the library.

That was completely rude by etiquette, but I understood his frustration. He thought of us as liars.

"Oliver?" I barely squeaked.

"We'll figure it out, Sof. Don't worry. Let's get you home."

Oliver led me to the front, where a carriage waited for us. Gabe must not have completely abandoned us. After I got into the carriage, I looked out the window and saw Gabe watching us from the second story. He seemed sad with his drooped shoulders and no sign of a smile. I put my hand up to wave goodbye, and he turned away.

CHAPTER

EIGHT

Arriving home at nearly suppertime with no energy left, I had to check on Chumana's egg. I needed to be sure it'd stayed warm enough.

Before we left the carriage, I asked Oliver, "How should we get the egg to the fire tonight? Are you okay to do that yourself? Or do you want me to stay up and come get it?"

"I can do it. Don't worry. I'll go straight to my room while you go distract Mother with tales of our day. Don't tell her it ended badly."

"Obviously. I'll just give her the nice details like him helping me from the carriage and walking me to the library and such," I said.

The carriage stopped, and we got out. I thanked the driver, and we walked up our little path to the house. I stopped. Oliver stopped next to me and raised an eyebrow.

"Is that Mother? Singing?"

"I think it is." Oliver tilted his head and furrowed his brow.

I instantly felt as if I were drowning. "She found it."

We ran for the door at the same time and swung it open, shoving each other to get inside.

"What on earth are you two doing?" Mother scolded.

I stood straight and smoothed my skirt. "Nothing, Mother. We thought we heard something, so we raced each other to the door."

"Well, you did hear something. How could you two keep this from me?" Mother demanded, placing a hand on her hip.

"Keep what from you, Mother?" Oliver asked.

"Oh, hush. You two are so sweet. How ever did you save up for it? I've heard of these things before but never thought we'd get one. Did the Thomases put you up to it? Is it a gift from them? Is it for you, Sofia, and you just didn't want to tell me? When is the wedding?" Mother skipped from foot to foot and clasped her hands to her chest.

I didn't know the Mother before me, but she sure was nice when she was happy. Neither Oliver nor I knew what to say to her. She had to have found the egg, but we didn't want to talk about it if she had intercepted something else we didn't know about.

"Where did you put it?" Oliver asked.

Ah. Well done, Oliver. Always the clever one.

"I thought you'd never ask. I'll show you." Mother twirled her skirt as she spun and led us into the little family gathering room.

As my eyes searched the area, Oliver grabbed my arm. There, on the little table in front of the seating area, sat Chumana's egg—exposed to our drafty air and not a source of heat to be found. I thought I would vomit.

"Sofia. You don't look very pleased. What is wrong with you? I thought you'd be ecstatic. Did the Thomases truly give this to you? Are you now engaged?" Mother asked.

I didn't know what to say. I just gaped at her. Oliver

seemed just as stunned as I felt as he opened and closed his mouth.

"Well?" the happy Mother was quickly fading.

"It's an odd gift, Mother. We're not sure where it came from, but it had a note that said it must be kept warm. I don't know if it's to keep that beautiful color or what the reason, but it must always be warm. Does it still feel warm, Mother?" My voice cracked.

Oliver's head snapped in my direction, then he quickly looked at the floor.

"Oh." Mother walked to Chumana's egg and laid her hands on it. "It does feel warm. How are we supposed to keep it warmer? I don't want it to lose that vibrant color."

"I believe the note said to put it in warm embers or even in a fire, if I recall," Oliver said.

Good. We were back on the same page. Oliver glanced at me sideways, and we both held back our smiles.

"Well, I'd better get this in the fire. I wouldn't want its beauty to fade." Mother scooped up the egg and hurried off.

Oliver and I released our breaths.

"Oliver, I'm so grateful to have you go through this with me. But what are we going to do?" I asked.

Oliver shook his head and shrugged. His eyes looked sad. "Sof, I think it may be time that you try to settle down with Gabe. He's not a bad guy. And he can help us."

I couldn't believe what I had just heard. My brother had never been pro suitor. He was always on my side.

"No, Sof. I don't mean to get rid of you or choose his side. Listen. I don't know why Gabe started calling on you now, but think about it. We don't know how long we have before that egg hatches. And we'll be doomed with a dragon around here. Gabe must have some connections or other homes that he could stash you and the dragon in for a year."

"Then what? I come home and pretend nothing happened? I know I'm difficult and stubborn, but I could never use somebody like that without feeling guilty."

"Then you have to decide what to do. That book said a dragon will only choose a worthy person. You won't fit in completely with dragons or humans. We need help. This is bigger than us. This is helping preserve dragons."

I closed my eyes to think and rubbed my temples. I wasn't ready to get married. I knew Mother was ready to marry me off, especially to someone wealthy, but I wasn't sure I could do it. Maybe Oliver was right. I needed help, and Gabe wasn't like the other suitors we'd met.

I opened my eyes and sighed. "Fine. I'll write him a note and see if he'll go for that walk he told Mother about. Hopefully, he is as kind as he seems and will still go with me."

"That sounds like a good place to start."

I HAD WRITTEN and sent off the letter asking Gabe for a walk the day before, and I still hadn't heard anything from him, good or bad. I worried that my brattiness had finally come back to bite me. The one person I had found who seemed halfway decent was angry with me. My thoughts wandered to Chumana, and I felt so incredibly guilty for my behavior. I had promised her I would take care of her baby, and already, I had failed my first task.

I moped around the house for a while, then since Mother had become a little less singsongy, I figured I would be better off outside. Maybe I could head to my swing to think about things. I grabbed my cloak because the air seemed to be cooling down as we approached fall.

Following my path, I realized that I needed to bring out

some hedge trimmers. The bushes grabbed at my cloak. Thank goodness I had snatched my old one from my mother's pile, so I wouldn't ruin my nicer one. I stopped at the place where Chumana had passed away. The brush was already growing back, and the grass she had lain on barely showed evidence that she had been there. I wondered if it had been chance or if she'd known it to be so close to my home.

"What are you doing?"

I screamed and jumped, tripping on my dress and falling flat on my rump. I looked up to see Gabe standing over me.

"Wha-what are you doing here?"

"Gee, it's nice to see you too. I'll see you later then." Gabe backed away.

"I'm sorry." I truly meant it.

He chuckled and reached out to me. "Come on. Ladies don't belong on the ground."

I smirked, relieved that he wasn't angry with me after all. I let him help me up then dusted off my cloak.

"Honestly, though, what are you doing here? I thought you were angry with me."

He didn't look angry, just amused.

"I was. At first, anyway. Then I realized you didn't know me, and I really didn't know you. I showed up at your house because my mother said, even if you weren't wealthy, you were pretty, and you'd make beautiful children. I did it just to appease her, as I'm sure you meet with suitors just to appease your mother. I understand that you have every right to not trust me. But once I realized that you weren't like every other girl, I knew I wanted to get to know you... for me... not for my mother."

My face must have spoken for me because he stopped and scratched his head.

"No, no. Not get to know you as a suitor and potential

bride. I want to get to know who you are and what you like. Sofia, I would like to be your friend," Gabe said, completely serious.

I could only say what felt right to me in that moment. "I'm not looking for a husband, but what I am looking for is someone who can help me."

"Help you? With what?" Gabe asked.

"That's the thing. I'm not entirely certain. We've been doing research at your house because... Oh, I don't even know how to say this without you thinking I'm a maniac. Well, maybe it'd be better if I showed you." I turned and pointed to the area where Chumana had been. "Do you see this flattened area?"

Gabe looked around, drawing his eyebrows together. "It looks like something big was here. What happened?"

I wished Oliver were with me. "A dragon was injured here. Well, not here, but she landed here to—"

"A dragon? Seriously? A real live dragon? I've only heard about them in stories." Gabe almost knocked me down as he moved forward, but he grabbed my arm to steady me. Then he continued past to look around. He grabbed a darkened leaf. "Is this... is this its blood?"

My heart hurt for her. "Yes. Her name was Chumana. She was a beautiful black dragon."

Gabe plopped down like a child and sat cross-legged on the ground. "Please, tell me more." He patted the ground for me to join him.

I took a few steps forward and sat across from him. "Why are you so interested, Gabe?"

"Who isn't interested in dragons?"

"Are you interested because you want to be a dragon hunter?" I had to be sure his intentions were good.

"What? Why would you think that? Why would I want to hurt a magical species?"

"A lot of people do. They want to kill them off because they think they're dangerous. Dragons eat livestock and bring fear to towns and villages. Why do you *not* want to hurt one?"

Gabe chuckled. "I understand your concerns, I truly do. But you won't fully trust me until I'm put to the test. However, I can promise that I would never want to harm a dragon. I've always been fascinated by the stories about them, and I would love for them to thrive again."

I couldn't help but smile. Gabe was right. Until I saw him in action, I would be suspicious of everything he said or did. I could only hope I was making the right decision.

"Gabe, I need to show you something. Something really important."

"What is it?"

"Come with me."

We entered through the back door of the house, and I hoped Mother wouldn't be too angry. She only ever made sure the front entry and sitting areas were tidy in case of visitors. The back of the house was my favorite because it felt like a home, not an entertainment parlor. I pulled Gabe in by his hand, and I walked us to the hearth. Mother had placed the egg in the very front of the fire.

"Is that...? No. There's no way—"

"Shhh. Only Oliver and I know what this truly is," I whispered.

"Oh," Gabe whispered back, never taking his eyes from the egg. "It's so beautiful."

"What's so beautiful?" Mother asked as she joined us. "Oh, Gabriel! It's a pleasure to see you here. I thought I heard Oliver talking. What brings you to our humble abode?"

My poor mother smoothed out her hair and dress as quickly as she could each time Gabe looked away from her.

"Well, hello there, Mrs. Taylor. Your beautiful daughter

brought me back here. She is quite the entertaining spirit. I thought perhaps she and I could spend some time together, if that's okay with you." Gabe gave her a dazzling smile.

"Oh, of course you may call on Sofia anytime you'd like. Our home will always welcome you. And thank you so much for the beautiful courting gift. How ever did you manage to find something like that?" Mother did a perfect curtsy.

Gabe glanced at me, and I inclined my head toward the egg.

"Thank you, Mrs. Taylor. I appreciate your kindness. As for the, uh, the courting gift... well, my family has been holding onto it for a promising match. My family agrees that we all enjoy Sofia's company, so we thought it was time to pass the gift on."

My heart skipped. Gabe was just as good at playing the game as Oliver and I.

"Oh, well, I am so pleased to hear it. Again, you are welcome here anytime." Mother curtsied again.

That time, she waited for Gabriel to incline his head, then she left.

I gaped at Gabe. "You really are good at this."

"I've been at it longer than you have." Gabe grinned. "So, what are we to do about this?"

"I don't know. Let's go back outside, where it's harder for anyone to eavesdrop."

We walked out back and headed down my trail again until we reached my swing.

"My favorite thinking place," I said.

"I can see why you like it. It's nice and private out here." Gabe looked all around the clearing.

"So, 'What are we going to do?' That's the question of today. Oliver and I have no idea what to do. Unfortunately, even your books didn't tell us a whole lot. The closest we found was that I will never be accepted by humans or dragons for helping Chumana's baby. I won't belong in either world. Though I've honestly never felt like I belonged in this world anyway. I just can't do the parties and the false niceties. It's exhausting."

To my surprise, Gabe laughed. "Sofia, you have the most amazing opportunity to get out of this world and maybe find one that fits you. You just don't see that yet because you are so focused on Chumana's egg. I think it's time to get Oliver and set out to see if we can find some dragons."

"Find some dragons? What about the dragon we do have? What are we to do with it?"

"Who better to ask how to care for a dragon than another dragon?"

I had to admit, Gabe was right. *But how would we find dragons?* They were lost to humans on purpose. The very fact that Chumana had landed right in my backyard was unheard of.

"Okay, let's find Oliver, then let's go find some dragons."

WE FOUND Oliver organizing the different bolts of fabric that our father stored off to the side of the house in his sewing workshop. The space wasn't large by any means, but it was big enough for our father to carry out his own successful business. Bolts of fabric covered nearly every inch of open space and lined the walls, sorted by color. It always reminded me of a rainbow when I walked in.

"Hey, Oliver. We have a question for you," I said as we came through the doorway.

Oliver's eyes darted between Gabe and me. "This doesn't look like good news. What are you two up to?"

"It is good news if you want it to be," Gabe said.

"Just spit it out, Sof," Oliver said, continuing to work.

"Well, we are going to try finding some dragons to help us with Chumana's baby. I have no idea when it will hatch or how to feed it except to release it where there might be rats. I don't know how to communicate with it or anything. We need help, so we are going to find it," Sofia said.

"And just how do you expect Mother to allow you out of the house? Especially unmarried," Oliver said.

"I thought maybe you could be our chaperone. If she found out I was going someplace with Gabe, we'd be set. You and I both know she wants me to marry him. Think of all the parties she could go to with our marriage."

Oliver stopped moving bolts of fabric around and crossed his arms. "What makes you think I want to go search for dragons? They'll eat me. Not one of us knows how to use a sword. And even if we took a sword or bow, we couldn't save ourselves against dragons."

I sighed. I hadn't really thought it through. I just knew I had to do it. I could feel it was the next step.

"Fine. If you don't want to help us, that's okay. I don't blame you. It could get scary, and I have no plan whatsoever beyond going to Gabe's to see if I can find the last known location of dragons. All I know is that I need to keep my promise to Chumana, and I will do whatever it takes to keep her baby safe. I'll be sure to say goodbye before we leave." I turned to Gabe. "Let's go."

As I reached for the door handle, Oliver said, "Sofia." He waited for me to face him. "You and I both know I can't let you do this alone. Sorry, Gabe, not alone, alone but without me. I'd never forgive myself if something happened to you."

"Oh, Oliver!" I bounded to him and wrapped him in a hug. "Thank you, thank you, thank you!"

"Don't thank me just yet. You need to figure out how to get

Mother to approve not only taking your egg but leaving for who knows how long."

I broke away from our hug. "I know. I figure I'll have to lie to her. I don't want to, but this is important."

"And don't forget me. We all know our mothers would love nothing more than a marriage for me and Sofia. I think we can use that to our advantage. What if we set up a carriage ride to our home in Carstel? They wouldn't protest us three going there for a few days, right? Just to show you our other home, maybe?"

"I think that's a great idea." I looked to Oliver for agreement.

I could tell he was considering the possibilities as he chewed his lower lip and his eyes searched the ceiling.

"Yes, I think we could make that work to our advantage," Oliver said.

"I think we need more dragon books, though, to find out where we should even start. Plus, we need to plan ways to keep the egg warm. What if we can't start a fire? Or are followed and don't want to give away our location? Then what?" I asked.

"All in good time. We'll begin our research, then we can get going. First, we need to convince our parents to let us take a little vacation to Carstel. Once we can get that underway, we can easily head in whichever direction we need to find some dragons," Gabe said.

"Sounds perfect. Gabe, if you don't mind, I'd like to accompany you to visit your library before we make more plans," I said.

Oliver smiled and gave me a single nod.

"Okay, my lady, we have some work to do."

THE RESEARCH TOOK LONGER than I had anticipated. To find a place to start seemed like searching for a needle among a thousand bolts of fabric. However, after two solid weeks of endless reading, we found where to begin. Ironically enough, Carstel had the last known dragon sighting, besides Chumana, of course. It had been around forty years since a dragon had been spotted there, but we figured that it couldn't hurt to ask around.

It also didn't take much effort to convince our parents to let me and Gabe go—with Oliver as a chaperone. They gave us that stipulation, so we didn't fight. In fact, it worked in our favor. I felt bad for deceiving Father. When I looked into his eyes, I could tell he knew we were lying, but he couldn't possibly have known why.

The day before our trip, Gabe, Oliver, and I were at my swing in the woods, planning the first part of our next steps. I sat on the swing while Gabe and Oliver stood in front of me.

"Carstel is about thirty miles away, so we should easily reach that in one day. We can go on our horses after that. Wait. Sofia, can you ride a horse like a man?" Gabe asked.

I had never actually ridden a horse. I'd always been in a carriage or cart. Mother had never pushed me to learn to ride. We didn't have a riding horse, only one that pulled our little cart.

"Well, no. But I'm sure I could manage if given enough time," I said.

"She's a quick learner, Gabe. You'll find that out soon enough. But learning to ride a horse takes time, Sof. You'll have some really sore muscles for a while," Oliver said.

"Oliver, I'll want to teach you sword and bow while we're in Carstel. It's a bigger town, but we have more land there where we can practice our skills," Gabe said.

"What about me? Don't you think I should learn how to use a sword or bow?" I asked.

Both boys looked from each other to me. I shrugged one shoulder at them.

"It definitely couldn't hurt to have three of us prepared to protect ourselves," Gabe said.

Oliver grinned at me. "I think it'd be perfect for you."

"Thank you. I look forward to my training," I grinned. I couldn't imagine swinging a sword or firing a bow accurately. "I know we have pretty much everything figured out, but my greatest fear is keeping the egg warm. I think, though, that if we keep a bag filled with down pressed snugly against the egg, it should stay warm between fire sittings. It works for chickens to keep their eggs warm, so it should work for a dragon egg, right?"

Gabe shrugged. "I don't see why not. And I'd rather have that than nothing."

"Good, because I already created the bag and packed it full of down. Father helped me create the bag. I told him Gabe's family wanted us to take the rock with us because it will open at the moment when we should be officially engaged," I said.

"Did he seriously believe you?" Oliver asked.

"I don't think so, but you know Father. He loves us and supports us no matter what we do. I haven't told Mother that the egg is coming with us yet. I wanted reinforcements for that task."

Oliver laughed. "I understand. We'll be there for you. I think we should leave it until the very last thing, though. Or just pack it up when she's not looking and tell her as we ride away."

"Don't forget, we're taking the carriage from here to Carstel to keep up with the story for our mothers. We can switch to riding once we leave Carstel. That way, our mothers won't lose it over you riding like a man," Gabe said.

"Good idea. Okay. Do you two feel as if we are all set to get going tomorrow? Any last things we should figure out?" I asked.

Oliver and Gabe shook their heads.

"I think we're set," Oliver said.

"Perfect. Then let's get some rest. We begin for real tomorrow."

TEN

The next morning, I didn't want to waste any daylight, though we planned to stop in Carstel. But we still had to load all our belongings into the carriage. I needed to get Chumana's egg in its down bag, and I wanted to do that before Mother woke up. I grabbed the bag that Father and I had sewn and went to the hearth to collect the egg. Thankfully, nobody else rose so early, so I hurriedly placed Chumana's egg in my bag.

"Don't worry, sweet thing. We'll take you to your kind, where you'll be safe." I pulled the drawstring tight at the top of the bag and carried her to Oliver's room.

Knocking on the door, I let myself in. "Oliver, why are you still in bed? We've got lots to do today."

Oliver groaned, pulled his blanket over his head, and grumbled at me.

"Fine. But when Gabe and I leave you behind, it's not my fault."

Oliver pulled the blanket down just enough to let me see his eyes. "You can't leave without me. I'm your chaperone."

"Then hurry up." I giggled and went back to my room.

I finished packing and lugged my few bags to sit by our front door. I figured that I shouldn't pack very much because we would be on the road, but I wanted it to look like we planned to stay in Carstel for a while.

"Are you all set, then?"

I turned to see Mother standing behind me. "Yes, I think so. I just need Oliver to get going."

"I'm here. Don't get a wrinkle in your skirt." Oliver gave Mother a one-armed hug.

I shook my head at him.

"What time will Gabriel be here?" Mother asked.

"Any minute. He said this morning so we wouldn't have to push the horses too hard and could let them travel at a leisurely pace," I said. "Oliver, do you need help getting your belongings?"

"Nope. I only have a couple of suitcases. You girls travel too heavy. Guys don't need much to be happy."

"I hope you brought your nicest things. I don't want Gabriel to think we're poor," Mother said.

"Of course I brought nice things, Mother. Even that pretty blue vest you had Father make for me. Speaking of, where is Father?"

"He's in the kitchen. I wanted to fix you a little something so we can eat together as a family before you go on your adventure."

I smiled at Mother. She was so happy the trip was happening. I wondered what she would think if she knew the true reasons we were leaving.

"Well, let's not keep him waiting, then." I led the way to the kitchen. "Good morning, Father." I kissed his cheek and took my place at the table, which showcased a hearty breakfast.

As I loaded different foods onto my plate, we carried on with small talk while we enjoyed our breakfasts.

"Well, are you two ready to head out?" Father asked.

I looked at Oliver and smiled. "I think we're ready. Just waiting on Gabriel."

"How long do you think you'll be gone?" Father asked.

"You know, I'm really not sure. Gabriel didn't give us a specific time frame. I suppose if I run out of clean laundry, we could head back." I grinned.

"Well, I hope that you stay long enough to win him over. You two really make a fine match. I never thought we'd find somebody who could enjoy someone so unladylike," Mother said.

"Um. Thank you?" I could tell Mother wasn't being mean because she sounded truly delighted. But it was an odd way to deliver a compliment.

I was saved by a knock on the door.

"Oh, that must be Gabriel." Mother smoothed her dress. "Why don't you go and answer the door, Sofia?"

"Yes, Mother."

I opened the door, and there stood Gabe.

"Good morning, Miss Sofia. Are you ready for our travels?" Gabe asked.

I dropped into a polite curtsy in case Mother was watching. "Yes, I believe I am. Please come in."

Gabe turned and waved to our driver. He then turned back to me. "Is this everything?"

"I believe so. Oh, wait. Oliver needs to grab his two bags. I'll go get him."

Once we had everything stacked by the door for the driver to load, I went and grabbed my bag with the egg in it. I'd left that one in my room so it wouldn't get hurt.

Mother and Father stood by the entryway. Mother's eyes

teared up. It made me think for half a moment of what it would be like if I were really going on a trip to get to know Gabe better and perhaps become his fiancée. I quickly shook that thought from my head. The trip was for dragons, and he seemed knowledgeable.

After everything was loaded, I gave Mother a quick hug, then I hugged Father and kissed him on the cheek. Even Father seemed emotional, with tears in his eyes. I wondered if I would see them again. *And if I do, will they still accept me as a dragon sympathizer? Could I ever come back?* The thought of never seeing my home again turned my stomach. Oscar rubbed against my legs, and I picked him up.

"I love you, Oscar. You be a good boy for Grandma and Grandpa, okay?"

Oscar purred then booped his nose against mine. I kissed his cheeks and handed him to Father.

"I love you all," I said.

"Travel safely, and we love you too," Father said.

Mother simply wiped her eyes and gave us a small wave. Oliver put his arm around my shoulders, and we walked to the carriage.

OLIVER, Gabe, and I, plus Chumana's egg sat in the carriage as it rocked and bumped along the road to Carstel. I looked out the window as we left our little house. Our town of Holltree wasn't big, but it was home. I'd never traveled away from it before except to assist Father with his visits to measure different clients. I'd always been back home before the sun set.

"Are you okay?" Gabe asked.

I half smiled and shrugged one shoulder. "I'll be okay. I'm

just nervous, I guess. I've never left home like this before, and now I don't know if I'll ever be back."

"Understandable. But hey, you've got two guys and a dragon to keep you company. How many girls from Holltree can say that?" Gabe smirked.

I laughed and shook my head then watched out the window until our little town was no longer visible.

After it being quiet for a long time, Oliver spoke. "So, our plan is to continue to research dragons and learn some sword and bow skills. How long will we stay in Carstel?"

"I don't want to be there too long. What if the dragon hatches? But we also need to at least be able to use a sword and bow," I said.

"It may not be a bad idea to have her egg hatch there, though, because then we can take it to alleyways with a large rat supply. What if we're on the road and don't have a way to feed it or ourselves?" Gabe asked.

Oliver laughed. "This sounds to me like not one of us has a clue what we're doing. Besides, how long can we keep our mothers at bay? We will need to leave Carstel before either of them decides to join us."

Gabe and I laughed.

"You're right, Oliver. I can't imagine what Mother would do if she showed up and we had a baby dragon. So I say let's train right away and see how far we can get. Also, I don't want to stay around town too long after we start asking questions," I said.

"I doubt we'll find any dragon hunters in Carstel," Oliver said.

"Yes, but we can't be too careful. What if word reaches some dragon hunter that we're asking around? Then what? It's not like we can fight our way to safety. Especially against dragon hunters. I imagine they're skilled in killing things," I said.

Gabe and Oliver nodded.

"We'll be careful. We can probably start with some of the older people in town. There are always storytellers around too," Gabe said.

"What good will storytellers do?" Oliver asked.

"They may only have tales, but some of them are old enough to have seen with their own eyes the stories they tell. We just have to find the right one," Gabe said.

"Well, let's train as quickly as possible so we can leave town once we get a lead," I said.

"That sounds like a proper plan. Once we get our lead, we'll know which direction to go," Gabe said.

"And perhaps the library you have in this house will help guide us. If Carstel had dragons, perhaps your family books will contain more recent information than some of the others we've looked at," I said.

"Let's hope so," Gabe said.

We all sat silently, lost in our own thoughts, for most of the trip. I wondered exactly how we would get everything done and leave before our parents caught on that we weren't coming back. It broke my heart to leave on a lie, but I knew it would be best for Chumana's baby. I stuck my hand inside the feather-filled bag. At least the egg was still warm. Our plan had worked so far.

CHAPTER

ELEVEN

My head banged against the back of my seat as the carriage came to an abrupt halt.

"Ow." I rubbed the back of my skull. "We must be here?"

I looked out the window at a beautiful mansion. It was even larger than Gabe's house in Holltree. It shared the same general shape, including arches complementing the doorways. The current house sat a little taller and had more stairs leading up to the front door. An immaculate row of hedges lined the stairs and curved around, creating a little barrier all along the front of the mansion.

"You can close your mouth." Gabe laughed.

I snapped my jaw shut. "This place is huge."

"It's home away from home. We have a full staff to take care of it while we're gone. They shouldn't bother us too much."

Oliver's eyes were wide with shock. Neither of us had ever been invited to a home so large.

The carriage door opened, and the driver held out his hand

for me. I figured I'd better at least try, so I took his hand and allowed him to help me out of the carriage. I nodded my thanks, and he went to unpack our luggage.

A tall, gray-haired, medium-set man in a finely tailored black suit opened the beautiful wooden doors. He must have been their butler.

"Gabriel, welcome back." The man opened his arms wide, a huge smile under his thick mustache.

"Harold, it's great to see you." Gabe rushed up to the man and wrapped him in a tight hug.

Odd.

Gabe faced us, his hand on Harold's shoulder. "Harold has been with me since I was a baby. Though I don't know why he still insists on calling me Gabriel. He'll help us with anything at all that we need."

I dropped into a curtsy. "It's a pleasure to meet you, Harold. If you have anything to do with the nice young man Gabe has turned into, you must be quite the role model."

"Thank you, madam. You're too kind." Harold inclined his head. "Let's get you all settled in. I'll have a bath drawn for you." Harold turned and snapped his fingers at two young ladies in maid dresses who stood in the doorway. They curtsied and left. Harold then gestured at a young, thin, brown-haired gentleman. "Andrew, let's get this luggage inside."

Andrew hurried over to the carriage and grabbed several bags.

"Gabriel, would you be so kind as to show our guests to their rooms?" Harold asked.

"Of course. Thank you, Harold." Gabe affectionately squeezed the man's arm and waved his hand for Oliver and me to follow.

I clutched my egg bag in my arms. I didn't want it to leave my sight.

"Do you ever get lost in here?" Oliver asked as Gabe led us down a long hallway.

Gabe chuckled. "I did when I was a kid, but Harold always seemed to know where I was. He can be super sneaky, so be careful what you say. Not that I don't trust him. I trust him completely. I just don't know who else might be around. We aren't necessarily ever alone."

"Well, how is that supposed to work?" All I could think of was what would happen if one of the house staff was around when Chumana's egg hatched.

Gabe must've read my mind. "Don't worry. Everyone here should be completely trustworthy. But Harold you can rely on. He's your man no matter what you need. Andrew is new, though, so I can't say much about him."

We finally arrived at my room, and Gabe opened the door for me. I couldn't get over how beautiful everything was. It all looked like it belonged in a royal castle. Gold covered the chairs, mirrors, and picture frames, just like their home in Holltree.

"Get settled in. A bathroom is attached, and I'm sure the maids have already drawn you a bath." Gabe pointed to a doorway that must have led to the bathroom.

"Thank you."

"No problem. Oliver's room is right next to yours, and mine is down the hall. We'll come get you for supper."

Gabe and Oliver left me. I closed the door and took in my room, which rivaled the size of my house. Windows stretched from floor to ceiling with sitting chairs on either side. Multiply my bed at home by three, and that was the size of my new bed. I wondered if my sister had felt as overwhelmed as I did in Gabe's home when she saw the size and beauty of her new home compared to our small one.

The two maids at whom Harold had snapped his fingers

appeared in my bathroom doorway. They both curtsied. They were almost identical in their small statures, except one was a brunette and the other was a blonde.

"We have your bath ready for you, madam," the brunette said.

"Thank you. I'm sorry, what are your names?"

They glanced sideways at each other then looked back at me.

The brunette said, "I'm Bridget, and this is my twin sister, Bella. We are at your service, madam."

"Thank you, Bridget. I should be okay for the rest of the evening if you want to take some time off."

Again, the two side-eyed each other. "Um. Yes, madam. We will be in the servants' quarters if you change your mind."

"Thank you, but I should be okay."

They both curtsied again and left my room.

I walked to the bathroom and was pleased that Bridget and Bella had already set a towel by the huge golden bathtub. I hurriedly undressed and dipped my toes in the water. It was perfect. After being bumped along the road for thirty miles, I couldn't wait to get in. I dropped into the tub, and all the tension released from my shoulders. I could definitely get used to that.

THE NEXT MORNING, we began our training. Gabe took us out to the courtyard, where three big sticks stood against the wall of his home.

"What are the sticks for?" Oliver asked.

"They're for training. You didn't think I'd hand you a sword on day one, did you?" Gabe laughed.

I smirked as Oliver said, "I suppose not."

"For today, I just want you to get used to holding something heavy and maneuvering it. I more or less want this stick to become an extension of your arm." Gabe handed Oliver and me each a stick.

The stick hadn't looked that heavy sitting against the wall, but as I held it, I realized it was about two inches in diameter and a lot weightier once I took it in a single hand. Gabe expertly swung his stick around in a circle. He then lunged and jabbed the stick forward.

"Today, let's work on swinging our swords in a circle with your wrist. Then we'll work on the lunge I just showed you," Gabe said.

Oliver and I shrugged at each other then swung our sticks in a circle. I dropped mine on the second rotation. Oliver laughed, and I glared at him.

"Shut up."

I picked up my stick and began circling it again. I dropped it on the third rotation. Oliver snickered. I retrieved it and tried again.

After my sixth drop, Gabe walked over and picked up my stick before I could kick it.

"We're building your muscle. This isn't a natural movement for you, and you've probably never held something heavy like this. Don't worry if you keep dropping it. I promise you won't forever." Gabe squeezed my shoulder and handed me my stick.

I took a deep breath and began again. The torture treatment felt like it went on for hours. Finally, Harold announced that lunch was ready. I'd never been so happy to end a task in my life. It was even more infuriating that Oliver could swing his stick around easily and had already moved on to the lunge-and-jab movement.

As we walked to the dining room, Oliver punched my arm

lightly. "Don't worry, kid. We can't all be excellent swordsmen."

I rolled my eyes and shook my head. "Hush, Oliver. I'll catch up to you."

"I doubt that," Oliver said.

"I don't know, Oliver. I haven't known Sofia long, but I feel like she'll stick to what she says," Gabe said.

I smiled at Gabe and held my head a little higher. He was right. If Oliver told me I couldn't do something, I would prove him wrong. Oliver shrugged a shoulder and kept walking.

After lunch, we went back out to the courtyard. That time, crossbows and arrows stood against the wall instead of sticks.

Gabe pointed away from where we'd entered the court-yard. "See those bales of hay? Those are our targets. Now, let's get to work."

Gabe handed us each a crossbow and a quiver full of arrows. He grabbed his own crossbow and showed us how to string it then pull the string back until it was cocked. I glared at Oliver as he pulled the string back with minimal effort. My arm still felt like jelly after all that fake-sword swinging. Oliver knew better than to laugh at me, though, because he looked away every time I glanced at him.

Finally, I got the string cocked. Gabe then had me grab an arrow and place it against the string without holding my fingers in front of the arrow, just in case the string released. Oliver had already cocked and released about half of his quiver of arrows. I closed my eyes to clear my head and took a few deep breaths. It wasn't a competition. I needed to learn how to use weapons for my own safety.

"Ready?" Gabe asked.

I nodded and stepped up next to Oliver so I could release my arrow from the same distance.

"You can get closer," Oliver said.

"I'm fine right here." I steadied my breathing and raised the crossbow.

"Just like that, Sofia. You're holding it perfectly. Now aim at the bale," Gabe said.

I held my breath as I pulled the trigger, then I lowered the bow to my side and looked toward my bale.

"You hit it! You hit it almost dead center! Did you see that, Oliver?"

I laughed. No way could I have hit it on the first try. Nearly a bull's-eye filled my soul after such a disappointing morning.

"That was a lucky shot. Let me see you do it again," Oliver said.

Still on a high from doing so well, I restrung my bow and placed my arrow. I closed my eyes for a moment, steadied my breathing, held my breath, then released. My arrow struck the bale just centimeters from my first.

"You're a natural. Go on. Do more arrows." Gabe plopped down on the grass next to me and handed me a new arrow after every shot.

I continued until I'd run out of arrows. The three of us walked down to my bale to find that every arrow had pierced the bale within six inches of each other, some splitting others.

"Well, I may not be able to use a sword well, but a crossbow, I can seem to manage."

I smirked at Oliver, who rolled his eyes then smiled and laughed.

"You truly are a natural. I can't wait to get you on a horse," Oliver said.

When it came time for supper, Oliver had begun to improve his crossbow shooting, and so had I. My arrows were all within three inches of each other. I had to shoot less at a time to avoid snapping the arrows. Gabe seemed pleased with my progress. He turned out to be quite the fine archer as well.

"I'm going to head to my room for a moment, then I'll join you boys in the dining area."

Gabe and Oliver nodded and headed for the dining room, and I turned down the long hall toward our rooms. I wanted to check on Chumana's egg. We planned to head into town the next day and ask around about dragon hunters to see what information we could find. But I had every intention of keeping the egg hidden, even from Harold, just in case.

I entered my room and closed the doors behind me. "Hello? Is anybody in here?" I never knew if the maids or someone else might be in my room. I peeked in the bathroom and didn't see anybody. I hurried to my bed and pulled back the pillows. There was Chumana's egg, still as beautiful as the first time I'd seen it. When I reached for it, the egg was still warm. In fact, it felt a little warmer than normal after lying in the down pillows. I'd better mention that to Oliver and Gabe.

I covered the egg again and made sure it was completely tucked in the down pillows. I had a few minutes before I needed to get down to the dining hall, so I went to the library. I passed Bridget in the hall just outside the library. When I inclined my head, she dropped into a curtsy. Then she resumed dusting the different picture frames along the wall. I was surprised Bella wasn't with her. It seemed the two were never far apart. I stopped short as I saw Bella sitting at a table in the library, looking over the books we had left open yesterday.

Bella looked up and gasped then sprang out of the chair, nearly knocking it over in the process.

"I-I'm sorry, miss. I didn't realize you were there." Bella dropped into the deepest curtsy I'd seen yet. She kept her eyes on the floor and didn't rise.

"It's okay, Bella. What were you reading?" I asked, though I knew.

She stayed in her curtsy. "I, well, I'm not the best reader, so I was looking at the pictures."

"You can stand, Bella. It's okay."

Bella lifted her eyes to mine for a moment, hesitated, then slowly rose to stand straight. She kept her head down.

"Why are you afraid?" I hadn't ever really been around servants but guessed that they weren't supposed to touch their boss's things.

"I'm sorry, miss, I just don't want to get in trouble. This is my first job as a maid, but I've always been curious," Bella said.

"Well, I won't say anything if you don't."

Bella lifted her eyes to me and grinned, her face flushed. "Thank you, miss. I won't forget this." She dropped into another deep curtsy then rushed from the room.

I walked to the book Bella had been looking at, and my heart lurched. There, on the page facing me, was a dragon that looked exactly like Chumana. The words on the opposite page read, "Chumana—last known female dragon—last seen outside of Carstel by local inhabitants—year 1801." That was forty years ago. *Would anybody who had seen her still be alive? They would if they had been young. Harold. Where did Harold grow up?* I had to find Gabe.

CHAPTER

TWELVE

I ran to the dining hall, figuring Gabe and Oliver should've arrived, and was thrilled that they were both there. They stood from their chairs as I rushed in, both with drawn eyebrows at my hurried entrance. Only the three of us were in the dining hall.

"Look! Look here. Read what it says." I shoved the book in front of them, the page open to Chumana.

As Gabe and Oliver read the passage, their eyes opened wide.

"It can't be," Oliver said.

"No, it can't. How is this possible?" Gabe asked.

"I don't know, but this was forty years ago. We need to speak to someone who lived here then and ask what happened. Gabe, I think you know exactly who to start with." I searched his face for understanding.

"Harold," Gabe said.

"Yes, Gabe?"

I gasped and spun, using my body to block the book. Gabe

handed it behind him to Oliver, who then set it on a dining chair.

"You always have a habit of being right where I need you," Gabe said.

Harold smiled, and I couldn't help but return it. He seemed so much like a father figure. I sure hoped Gabe was right that we could trust him.

"Well, did you all need something? Or you just wanted to see if I would pop up at the right time like when you were a child?" Harold tilted his head, waiting for our reply.

Gabe laughed first, then Oliver and I joined him. I could see why Gabe was so taken with the man.

"Harold, we were wondering how long you've actually lived in Carstel," I said.

"Hm. How long have I lived in Carstel? Let's see. I was born not far from here, then I moved here prior to caring for your father, Gabe. So I'd say I've been here nearly fifty years?" Harold rubbed his chin as he looked toward the ceiling.

Gabe, Oliver, and I exchanged quick glances. I could barely contain my excitement. That was our first step to finding dragons.

"Things must've been a lot different then," Oliver said.

I couldn't help but grin. Oliver had led into the conversation seamlessly.

"Oh, yes, they were. The times weren't as easy as they are now."

"Why not?" Gabe asked. "Come, sit. Let's talk about this over supper."

"I cannot join you at a meal, Gabriel," Harold said.

"Well, aren't I in charge when Father isn't here? I say you can. None of us will tell Father, and if anybody else says anything, then we will vouch for you and say we made you," Gabe said.

Harold sighed. "Very well."

He came over, and we all sat, us three across from him.

"Well, when I was a much younger man, I came here to learn how to be a better butler. My father was a butler, so I wanted to be like him. Your family was the first one that hired me. However, they were dark times. The food was scarce, and dragons made it scarcer still—"

"Dragons? They truly existed?" I asked.

"Yes, dear girl, they did. Hunters from around would travel here to try their best to kill one."

"Why here?" Gabe asked.

"Because it was said that the mountains to the north were where the dragons thrived. They had a hidden cave somewhere up there. No human ever found it. My guess is that the dragons could somehow disguise it, or maybe the scouts were killed. It's hard for anybody to know for sure."

"But if the dragons could be safe in the mountains, why did they come down here?" I asked.

"Well, to eat. We always kept an eye to the sky. Sheep used to thrive here until the dragons came. Even today, people are afraid to keep livestock around here for fear that if they do, the dragons will return."

"I thought dragons were extinct," Oliver said.

"Nobody wants to risk it. They're afraid that if they bring the livestock back, the dragon populations will grow. Now, if you have questions about dragons and not my history, I'd be glad to tell you." Harold grinned.

We three chuckled nervously.

"We want to know both. I mean, who isn't interested when dragons are mentioned?" Gabe asked.

"Very well. I'd never seen a dragon up close until the one showed up. I'm guessing it's what you found in that book you're hiding." Harold raised his eyebrow at Oliver.

Oliver sheepishly pulled the book out from under the table and opened it to Chumana's photo. He turned it to face Harold.

Harold let out a whoosh of air. "Oh, yes. Chumana. She was a beauty. I don't think she intended to harm anybody here. I think she wanted peace but wasn't sure how to accomplish it. Dragons saw humans as dragon killers, and humans saw dragons as livestock stealers. We couldn't find a way to thrive together. It was always just war."

"What happened to her?" I asked.

"Well, she came to town and tried to speak to the people. I was young then but still had a healthy fear of dragons. I kept back a ways so she couldn't see me, and I watched the whole situation from around the corner of a building. She even tucked her wings to make herself look as small as possible. She seemed to handle the screaming crowd well until someone threw a spear at her that gashed her shoulder. She then let out a roar of pain and scared everyone who had gathered. I am not even sure to this day what happened then—just that she roared, set the building nearest her on fire, then flew away. I don't think she intended to hurt the town, but it still happened. No dragon has been seen since. It's as if they vanished. Dragon hunters showed up for years after trying to find the dragons' lair. They always went north because that was the direction Chumana had flown away."

"How long did it take for people to quit hunting?" Gabe asked.

"I'd say at least twenty years. But with no dragon sightings, the hunters eventually gave up. They'd often go to the pub, get drunk, and start trouble, so the town was glad when they stopped trying," Harold said.

"Did you ever want to find a dragon?" Gabe asked.

Harold laughed. "No. It did cross my mind, but after seeing Chumana, I was even more respectful of their size and knew that I was no hunter. However, I was a scholarly lad, and I researched dragons. That is part of why your family has so many books on them, Gabe. Did you notice the author of that one you're holding, Oliver?"

Oliver closed the book, and his jaw dropped. He turned the cover to face Gabe and me.

"Harold? You wrote that? I didn't know you were a writer!" Gabe said.

"And researcher. However, I found just as many dead ends as everyone else. All I know is you'll need a lot more than a sword and crossbow to defeat a single dragon, let alone a whole hoard." The corners of his mouth rose in a knowing grin.

I bit my lip. Surprisingly, Gabe's face turned red, and Oliver looked at his lap. Each of us shifted in our seats. We'd already been found out in our very first questioning.

"We weren't planning on hunting dragons, Harold." I checked that no other servants had entered. "But we plan on finding them."

Harold scoffed. "Why on earth would you do that? With them gone, the world has known peace."

Gabe gave me a single nod.

"Because we need to return something to them," I said quietly and grimaced, waiting for a verbal lashing.

The doors opened, and a kitchen staff member announced, "Dinner is ready."

Harold had already stood, and he bowed. "If you need anything, please let me know."

"Thank you," all three of us said as he left, and the kitchen staff wheeled in trays of food.

Harold had given us a lot to think about, and we ate in silence.

We decided to go to my room after supper. It probably wasn't the most appropriate place to meet, but we knew the maids would only come through my front doors, and we would have plenty of time to quiet, since the maids knocked before they entered. We sat in the chairs in front of the big windows.

"What do we do with this information? Harold confirmed the dragons were here, but he also said that hunters stopped coming because the dragons disappeared. I feel like we've barely begun, and we've already hit a dead end," Oliver said.

"I completely disagree. Harold gave us an excellent place to start. We head north to the mountains. Perhaps the dragons just need one of their own to come out of hiding," I said.

"But the north mountains aren't close. They take days to get to," Gabe said.

"Well, I guess we could stop and camp and continue practicing our sword and crossbow training. At least we'll be moving forward. Oh! And I need you to feel Chumana's egg. I swear it's getting warmer, and I haven't even put it in the hearth yet."

I went to my bed and pulled the egg out from under the down pillows. It felt even warmer than I thought it had earlier. I brought it to Oliver and Gabe, who put their hands on it.

"That definitely feels warmer than a few days ago. Do you think it's getting ready to hatch?" Oliver asked.

I shrugged. "That's the only thing I can figure. Another good reason for us to get on the road."

"Except for finding it food. It's a lot easier to feed a dragon in a town with rats or even the meat here than it will be in the wild," Gabe said.

"But Chumana said it'll be able to hunt for itself right away. Maybe it can help us hunt if we need more food," I said.

We sat in silence for a while, and I pondered what we should do next.

"Oh, Gabe... Are your servants illiterate?" I asked.

Gabe drew his brows together and pursed his lips to the

side. "I guess I'm not really sure. I've never vetted our servants. Father or Harold has always done that. Why do you ask?"

"Well, I was thinking about all the books we've left open in the library. I was wondering if we should be more careful about what we leave out for anybody to read. They might put everything we're doing together and tell a dragon hunter."

"Sometimes it's nice to have illiterate people in service because they can't read your private correspondences. I can ask Harold if it'd make you feel better," Gabe said.

"No, no, that's okay." It probably would have made me feel better, but I didn't want to raise suspicion. Bella hadn't been anything but kind to me, and I really had no reason to doubt her. I still felt like something was off, but I couldn't quite figure out why.

"I think we should start planning our departure," Gabe said.

Oliver and I nodded agreement. As we discussed what to bring and how to bring it, my mind wandered from Bella to what would happen if we actually did find the dragons. *What then? And what would happen when Chumana's egg hatched? Would it be good? Bad? Would the dragons come find us?* Maybe it would be good to move away from the larger population as soon as possible. I held Chumana's egg on my lap, and it felt even warmer. The egg was going to hatch. And soon.

THIRTEEN

Three days later, we were ready to leave. Harold stood on the front steps as he directed servants on what to load and where to load it. Gabe, Oliver, and I each had our own horse to ride, so we were trying to evenly fill our saddlebags with supplies. Chumana's egg remained in its bag, and I wouldn't let anyone near it. I side-eyed Bella a few times as she tried to see what was inside. Nonchalantly, I turned my body to block her view.

Harold came to bid us goodbye, and I hugged him.

"Thank you for everything, Harold. You truly are one of a kind, and I appreciate how much you've done for us."

He cleared his throat and smiled. "It was no trouble at all, little miss. I do hope that you'll come back to us soon."

"Thank you, Harold. We'll be back soon enough, I think." Gabe also hugged the older gentleman.

I smiled at our odd group. Gabe's best friend was his household butler. Oliver was the most proper of us and shook Harold's hand.

The stableman helped me up onto my horse, a beautiful

brown quarter horse with a black mane and tail and a white star on his forehead.

"Thank you," I said to the stableman.

He nodded then stepped back once both my feet were properly in their stirrups.

I hadn't had a lot of training on riding a horse, but I could manage well enough to stay in the saddle if we had to get away fast. That seemed to be Gabe's biggest concern, which suited me because that was my biggest concern too.

With a final wave to Harold, we were off, Gabe and Oliver riding on either side of me. I turned to see Bella staring after us. Harold beckoned to her, and she went back into the house. Something still didn't feel right, but I had never spoken to Harold about her. If he trusted her, then I hoped she would be okay.

I turned my attention back to the road ahead of us. Things were going to get interesting, especially if Chumana's egg decided to hatch soon.

"What are we supposed to name Chumana's baby? Do you think dragons just come with names? Do they receive names after a while? I don't recall dragon naming in any of our research," I said.

Oliver laughed. "I imagine we'll find out soon."

I placed my hand inside the bag I wore against my chest, and Chumana's egg was roasting. "I wonder if I should take it out of the down. It's really hot."

"Let's get as far away from town as possible. We can assess the egg's heat when we find a place to camp," Gabe said.

Oliver and I agreed, but I worried that the egg would hatch a lot sooner than that. We avoided town, taking the road alongside it that led north. We really didn't want to be seen. *Who knew who might be in town just waiting and watching?* It was better not to risk the exposure.

As soon as we'd ridden about a half mile out of town toward the northern mountains, it became obvious that the road was rarely used. Tall grass covered the path. Branches from the brush and younger trees alongside the edges stretched their fingers, trying to grab us as we passed. Our horses pushed together so close our legs almost touched.

"Well, this isn't very comforting." Oliver attempted a laugh.

I'd thought the same thing and gave a half-hearted laugh. Even Gabe chuckled nervously.

"Do you think it'll be like this the whole way?" I asked.

"I imagine it's only going to get worse the farther we get from town," Gabe said.

I adjusted myself in my saddle and reached into the bag. Chumana's egg was even warmer.

"You guys, I don't think we're going to have time to reach a camping spot before this egg hatches. I think we'll be meeting Chumana's baby sooner than later," I said.

Gabe and Oliver tried peering into the bag.

"It's getting hotter. I sure hope it doesn't scare the horses." My chest tightened at the thought of losing the dragon and my horse at the same time. I wasn't sure I had the skills to keep a horse and a dragon calm.

"We'll do what we can to keep it from scaring them. They shouldn't spook too easily, though. Father doesn't waste money on useless things, so these horses are well trained," Gabe said.

I hoped he was right. Oliver clenched his jaw, but he nodded at Gabe. We carried on in silence, knowing our goal was to get as far from town as possible. We were only about two miles down the road when the bag moved.

"Um. You guys? We need to get off the road right now," I said.

"Where are we supposed to go?" Oliver asked.

The brush was dense all around us without the slightest opening to suggest a place we could get off the road. We really had no place to go.

"Let's tie the horses right here, then we can walk up the road a bit. That way, if somebody comes by, the horses will make noise and alert us," Gabe said.

We dismounted and tied our horses to the branches that hung closest to us over the road. The egg wiggled enough that I feared I would drop the bag. It felt as though it was trying to spin circles. I clutched the bag tightly so the egg wouldn't fall out. Oliver put his hand on my back and pushed me forward, away from the horses. We were lucky enough to be around a slight bend to block the horses from view. I carefully placed the bag on the ground and looked to Gabe and Oliver for guidance. Their faces remained blank, and I realized we were all equally clueless.

"Maybe I better take the egg out of the bag in case it kicks out on the bottom." I reached in and pulled out the egg.

We stood in a triangle around the egg as it rocked forcefully. No cracks appeared on the shell, but the little dragon clearly couldn't wait to get out. I wanted to keep the egg steady on the bag but also didn't want to be holding it when the dragon busted through.

"Look!" Gabe pointed.

Oliver and I joined Gabe on his side of the egg, and sure enough, an obvious white crack ran along the shell, which constantly changed color. I gasped and covered my mouth. Chumana's baby was almost there. I dropped to my knees, wanting to be the first thing the baby saw when it arrived. The fissures grew from the original crack, like a spiderweb. Oliver and Gabe dropped on either side of me as we watched the seams continue to spread.

After several minutes, the center of the web popped open, the shell landing a few inches from the egg. A little black leg with tiny black claws stuck out of the hole.

"Welcome to the world, little one." I resisted the urge to touch the leg. I wanted the baby to hatch as much as it could by itself.

The dragon's leg jerked back in at the sound of my voice. I hoped I hadn't scared it. A little green eye that resembled my cat Oscar's peered at me through the hole. If a dragon could squint, I swore it did, then it stared at me.

"Hello, little one. My name is Sofia. I'm a friend of your mother, Chumana."

The eye continued to stare at me as I spoke. Then it disappeared. A little grunt followed, then two feet appeared at the hole. The next thing I knew, the egg broke open, and the little black dragon somersaulted straight into my lap. All three of us gasped, and the dragon gave a startled grunt. I had instinctively caught the dragon in my hands, and as it uncurled its little body, no bigger than a kitten, it stared at me again. It cocked its head to the side and made little gurgling noises.

"I think it's hungry." I remembered Chumana saying that, upon its birth, it would need to feed. "Let's see if we have some meat to give it."

The dragon whipped its head toward our horses and growled. It hopped unsteadily onto its feet, and the little black spikes along its spine stuck straight in the air, much like a surprised cat.

I looked in the direction the dragon was staring and found nothing out of the ordinary. "What's the matter, little one?"

Gabe and Oliver shrugged, both looking the same direction the dragon did.

"Well, well, well, what a surprise we have here," a man said as he came around the corner, aiming a crossbow at us.

FOURTEEN

I clutched the dragon to my chest. It continued to growl, facing the man, but, surprisingly, didn't try to get away from me.

"What do you want?" Gabe asked, his voice stern and unwavering as he stood.

"What do you think I want, kid? I've been after a dragon my whole life, and now you've got one—a baby at that. Do you have any idea what people can do with a dragon if they get it as a hatchling?"

I swore I'd seen the man somewhere before. "Who are you?"

The man turned his attention to me and grinned, revealing yellowed teeth under his scruffy blond mustache and patchy beard. His grimy tan shirt looked like it hadn't been washed in weeks. I wondered how long he'd been without a home or shelter. The growling little dragon at my chest stopped me midthought.

"Nobody you know," he said.

"No, I'm pretty sure I know you," I said. He looked so familiar. Actually, when I thought about it, he looked just like a male version of Bella—blond hair, same stature, but masculine. "Are you Bella's father?"

The man startled, and the crossbow wavered, allowing me, Gabe, and Oliver to leap into the brush. I'd hated the brush when we first set out, but I was grateful for it as we hid. Oliver pressed his finger to his lips then pointed for me to keep going deeper into the tangled mess. Gabe and he then gestured that they would try to get behind Bridget and Bella's father.

"You can't hide from me, you rats. I've lived in this area for years. I know every hiding place. Bella told me you'd be up this way. All I had to do was wait. That girl is clever, you know. She can't read, but she pieced everything together. And with your quick departure to the north, that was enough for her to alert me. Now, if you hand over that wee dragon, no harm will come to you. If you resist, however, I'll be forced to kill you all."

The little dragon continued to growl and stare in the direction of the man's voice. *How did it know he was bad?* I couldn't see Gabe or Oliver anymore. I just moved forward as quickly and as quietly as possible while keeping my head low, beneath the grass and brush.

"How about we kill you then continue on our merry way?" Gabe called, sounding farther away than the man.

I wondered if he'd circled around behind the horses and had gone on the other side of the road. *Is he armed?* I couldn't remember. *Did Oliver have a chance to get to his crossbow?* Gabe and Oliver would be no match unless they could hunt the hunter.

Nobody spoke, and my breathing sounded like a windstorm. I feared that Bella's father would find me any second. I looked down at the little dragon. What a way to welcome it into the world. It watched all around us but had stopped growling. It wiggled in my arms, but not too badly, trying to get a new vantage point. I found a hollow under a tree to crawl into.

"Ba."

I jumped. The dragon whipped its tail back and forth. *Did it just speak?*

"Was that you? If it was, please be quiet until we get away from the bad man," I whispered.

The dragon flicked its tail, cocked its head, and stared at me, but it didn't make another noise.

A scream pierced the air, and it took all my power to stay put. I couldn't tell who it had come from.

"Where's the dragon?" Bella's father yelled.

"Far from you." Oliver's voice cracked.

He'd shot Oliver. Tears fell down my cheeks, but I couldn't move. I couldn't risk all of us. *Could I? Would Oliver understand? Would he think I should go after him?* We hadn't talked at length about being in that kind of position.

I looked down at the dragon. "I need you to hide in my pouch. Do you understand?"

The dragon blinked twice and crawled into the pouch on the front of my shirt.

"Thank you. We need to go help my brother."

I crawled out of the hollow and realized that I wasn't entirely certain how far away I was. I would just have to follow the voices and stay down.

"Tell me where the dragon and your little friends are, or I'll kill you." Bella's father spoke through clenched teeth.

"We both know you won't keep us alive if we hand over the dragon," Oliver said, his voice holding firm.

Bella's father laughed. "Yeah, you're probably right. But I'll give you a quick and painless death if you help me."

Oliver scoffed. "Well, it's too late for that since you put an arrow in my leg."

Oh, Oliver. But please keep him talking. Where is Gabe?

"Yes, I suppose you're right. Sorry, pal."

Bella's father snorted, and Oliver grunted.

I circled around behind them and approached the horses. My horse saw me, and bless it, it didn't move. I grabbed my crossbow, quickly strung it, and crept back into the brush, looking for the best vantage point to see Bella's father. I had only made it a few yards into the brush when a hand touched my shoulder. I swung my crossbow around, and Gabe caught it. He held his finger to his lips then pointed for me to go back toward the horses. I backed up as Gabe started into the brush.

"Well, since your friends just abandoned you, I guess I have to make you scream so they—"

A gasp and solid thud was followed by a grunt.

"He's dead!" Oliver shouted.

I ran to Oliver and reached him just as Gabe did. An arrow protruded from Bella's father's back as he lay face down, blood pooling around him.

"Help me get this arrow out of my leg." Oliver gritted his teeth.

I dropped to his side. "I'm not sure how to take out an arrow."

"It's okay. I can help him. But, Oliver, I think we need to send you back to Carstel. I want you to take Bella's father so Bella and Bridget can bury him properly. He may have been a greedy bastard, but he's still their father. And make sure Harold fires them both," Gabe said.

"But what if Bridget had nothing to do with it?" I asked. She'd never made me feel uncomfortable like Bella had.

"Can't risk it. It'd only be a matter of time before Bella convinced her to spy on us or something."

"Um. Arrow. Leg. Can someone fix this?" Oliver held onto his thigh.

"I'm so sorry, Oliver. Gabe, please help him."

"Where's the dragon?" Oliver asked then sucked in air and groaned when Gabe broke off the arrowhead.

"Brrrp?" The dragon peeked its head out of my pocket.

All three of us laughed at the odd little thing.

"I'm sure going to miss seeing you grow up. Ah!" he howled as Gabe pulled the arrow free.

"Sorry, Oliver. I figured it'd be best to pull it while you were sidetracked."

"Thanks, Gabe." Oliver rolled his eyes. "Mother is going to kill us, you know."

"I know. But I have to keep on. You know I have to," I said.

"Well, maybe you just go and heal at Carstel, then. Your mother never needs to know that you didn't continue with us," Gabe said.

"That could work. For a while. Until she comes to find us, which I figure she'll do sooner or later," Oliver said.

"We'll get you bandaged up, then you can take Bella's father back. We will try to send word as often as we can," Gabe said.

The little dragon growled.

"I bet you're starving." I stood to find some food that was supposed to be Oliver's portion.

I handed a few strips of jerky to the little dragon, and it scarfed them down then sniffed my fingers for more. It ate a block of cheese and a few more pieces of jerky. As it smacked its lips, I noticed its droopy eyes and giggled. Just like a baby. Eat then sleep. It curled up inside my pocket.

While I had fed the dragon, Gabe had bandaged Oliver's leg. Oliver groaned as Gabe helped him onto his horse. Gabe then hoisted Bella's father onto the horse he'd found not far behind our own and strapped him down.

"I'd avoid town if I were you. Just follow the same route we took, and you should be okay."

Oliver nodded silently. He grimaced as he adjusted in the saddle.

"I love you, Oliver. Thank you for going on this journey with us. I'm sorry you won't be able to continue, but I'll write you when I can."

"I love you too, Sof. I'll try to keep Mother off your back as long as possible."

We both chuckled, and I patted Oliver's good leg. Then Oliver and Gabe said goodbye, and Oliver left us. I held back my tears until he was out of sight. I didn't want him to know just how bad it hurt to watch him leave. We'd never been apart for more than a day, and not that I didn't trust Gabe, but my brother had always been there for me. He'd even taken an arrow for me.

Gabe put his arm around my shoulders and rubbed my arm. "It'll be okay. Harold will take good care of him. Then he can be our liaison in Carstel."

I looked down at the little dragon sound asleep in my pocket. I should've had Oliver help me name it before he left.

"We should hide the egg remnants then get going. I bet the little guy would like to sleep in that down bag too," Gabe said.

"I didn't even think of that. It'd be so much warmer in there."

With a few grunts of protest, the little dragon moved into the bag. Once it seemed to realize how much warmer it was there, I didn't hear another sound. Gabe and I caught each other's eye and giggled. However, the mirth was short-lived. We had a dangerous mission ahead of us and one less person. Gabe's solemn expression reflected my feelings.

"We should get moving if we want to make good time. And with Bella's father knowing about us, I'm sure it won't be long before others find out. Bella will surely want revenge for her father's death," Gabe said.

I felt sick. *Who knew how many others she would send after us?* Gabe and I got our horses ready, climbed into our saddles, and proceeded toward the north mountains again. We didn't speak as we traveled, alternating trotting and walking our horses. His mind must have swirled as much as mine. All our plans had involved Oliver. *What would we do without him? How could we manage with just two of us?* Mother had finally wormed her way into my head, as I found traveling unaccompanied with Gabe a little uncomfortable and inappropriate. I shrugged off the feeling and tried not to think about Mother or being improper. The dragon world needed us. Chumana's baby needed us.

We rode for hours, only stopping to check our horses, and finally, the sun began to set.

"I think we should set up camp. Let's look for an area away from the road," Gabe said.

Gabe led the way, and we finally found a little area open enough that we could make camp. We tied the horses off to the side, leaving a fifteen-square-foot clearing. No trees hung over the spot, so we could even start a little fire.

"You sleep first. I'll keep watch," Gabe said.

I was so tired, I didn't argue. I handed him the bag with the still-sleeping dragon and found my bed on the grass. I fell asleep as soon as I shut my eyes.

FIFTEEN

A snake hissed close to my face. I jerked upright, and a little black blob landed in my lap. I realized it was the dragon. Gabe laughed as I snatched the dragon to my chest.

"Are you okay, little one?" I petted the spikes standing straight up on its back, trying to soothe the baby.

"Are you kidding me? That little monster tried to attack me when I went to wake you." Gabe laughed and took a few steps back. "It's like you've got your own guard dragon."

"I think we should name the guard dragon. But I don't know if it's a he or she." I held the dragon out in my palms. "Are you a boy?"

The dragon hissed and whipped its tail from side to side.

"Girl then?"

The dragon made a sound that resembled a purr and proudly raised its head.

"Girl it is! So what's your name? Do you have one? Or do we name you?"

The dragon stood on my hands and stared at me, unmoving.

Gabe chuckled. "Well, that's helpful."

The dragon turned to growl at him.

Gabe lifted his hands in surrender. "I meant no disrespect. We just can't understand you if you don't talk."

The dragon swished her tail and turned to continue staring at me. Her gaze made me uncomfortable, but I also felt like she was trying to tell me something.

"Your mother's name was Chumana. Are you supposed to take that name?"

The dragon shook its head.

Gabe shrugged and started packing our things.

"Well, aren't you helpful?"

Gabe laughed and continued packing.

I held the dragon back up in front of my face and searched for any sign of what to call her. She stared at me, unmoving.

"Well, we can always change your name later. I think I'll call you Brenyx. What do you think?"

The dragon tilted her head, then I swore she nodded. She circled once in my palms and purred again, raising her tail high in the air.

"I think she likes it." Gabe smiled. "Brenyx it is."

Brenyx ran up my arm and circled my shoulders. She wrapped her tail around my neck and perched on my right shoulder.

"You're such a good girl," I said.

Brenyx purred and kept her tail wrapped around my neck as I helped Gabe pack our belongings. She had remarkable balance and just clung to me tighter with her tail if I bent over too quickly.

"I think we still have at least two days before we'll reach the north mountains. We should probably try to hunt along the way to feed Brenyx and ourselves. I know we've got food, but it'd be best to not eat it all and run out on our trip home," Gabe said.

"If we even make it home." I had an uneasy feeling that the north mountains would be fatal.

We'd already lost Oliver to an arrow. *For his life, I'm grateful, but what other dangers will we face?*

"Way to be positive, there, Sof." Gabe smirked.

I flushed. "Sorry. I don't mean to be negative, but I already lost my brother, and we've barely begun."

"Understandable, but let's try to be positive so we don't get consumed by bad thoughts."

I nodded. "I can do that. So you think we have at least two days' travel?"

"Yes. At least. I'm not sure exactly how far we went before our interruption, so I lost track of time. But based upon where we are, it'll probably be that long, maybe half a third day."

Brenyx tilted her head at Gabe every time he talked as if trying to understand him.

"Is he interesting, Brenyx?"

At her name, she looked at me with her big green eyes. She gave me a little rumble then turned her attention to Gabe again.

"I think she's trying to decide if you're okay or not. You did basically attack me to wake me up, you know."

Gabe and I laughed, and Brenyx shifted on my shoulder. She didn't seem too sure of what to think about the sound.

"Sorry, Brenyx. That's called laughter. Humans make that noise when something is funny," I said.

Brenyx stared at my lips as I spoke. She did a little shimmy step on my shoulder then turned her attention to the road. I looked where she looked but saw nothing. She scampered down my chest and onto my saddle. I barely had time to grab her before she tried to leap to the ground.

"What is it?" I asked as she wriggled in my hands. Stopping my horse, I dismounted then set Brenyx on the ground.

She took off into the tall grass.

I panicked. "Should I chase after her?"

Gabe dismounted and checked the grass where Brenyx had disappeared. "No."

"Why not? What if we lose her? She's just a baby!" My knuckles turned white as I gripped my horse's reins.

What felt like an entire afternoon must have only been moments, and Brenyx popped out of the tall grass, clutching a mouse in her mouth. She pranced over, tail held high, dropped her mouse at my feet, then sat, tail twitching.

"I think she brought you a gift," Gabe said.

"Oh! You're such a good little hunter! Good job, Brenyx! I'm so proud of you!"

Brenyx stood and circled my legs in a figure eight, then sat in front of her mouse.

"You can eat it," I said.

Brenyx snorted at me. Gabe shrugged one shoulder. I racked my brain, trying to recall all the information we'd learned.

"Oh, I know! She wants us to cook it. She doesn't have her flame yet, and they prefer a little scorch to their meat. Am I right?" I looked at Brenyx for validation.

She purred and nodded.

"Gabe, we need a small fire."

Gabe looked around. "We should probably get off the road. Let me look for a small clearing."

I grabbed Gabe's horse, holding onto its reins while Brenyx and I waited for him to scout a place for a small fire. Brenyx dutifully picked up her mouse to wait for Gabe's return. Her eyes had followed his departure, and she continued to stare at the area he had disappeared into. Soon, the brush parted, and Gabe reemerged.

"I found a good little spot. Come on." Gabe waved for us to follow and turned around.

Brenyx trotted after him, her tail high and her mouse proudly on display in her mouth. The horses didn't seem to be bothered by her at all, which I was grateful for. Gabe had, in fact, found a perfect little area. Brenyx set her mouse in front of her and waited while Gabe started a fire.

Once Gabe roasted Brenyx's mouse, she ate it in a few fast bites, and we continued on.

"This is going to be a long trip if we have to start a fire every time Brenyx is hungry." I grinned at the little dragon perched on my shoulder once more.

"Well, let's just hope she doesn't need to eat that often. That mouse was nearly the size of a rat. She should be satisfied for a little while. We can give her some of our food too. I still plan on hunting."

Gabe, the man of reason. I was so glad he had strutted into my life at the request of his mother. I wasn't sure what I would've done without his library, his help, or him.

WE DIDN'T HAVE to stop again until nightfall. I was terrified to reach the north mountains, but I hoped that Harold had been right and we would find dragons there. Nobody had seen a dragon in years, but they had flown to the north. *Will we have to travel many more miles over and beyond the mountains?* Brenyx, who still loved her place on my shoulder, stared north, even as we sat by our little pile of sticks, dry grass, and leaves we'd collected for a fire. It was like she knew where we were going. *Or is she being called toward her home?*

"Do you think dragons have a natural sense of where home is?" I asked Gabe.

He looked at Brenyx then me and scrunched his face. "I guess I'd never thought about it. But based on the way she's been staring north ever since we started, maybe they do? Or it could just be that she's looking the way we're heading."

"I don't think she's looked behind us once, though."

Gabe and I continued to watch her. Brenyx cocked her head at me as if to say "What?" then looked north again.

"Do you think she'll learn to communicate?" Gabe asked.

"I do. Chumana spoke to me just fine. And when Brenyx was freshly born, she made some noise that sounded kind of human. I don't know why she hasn't tried again since."

If a dragon could have a blank expression, Brenyx did. It really was odd, though, that she had attempted a human noise upon birth but then not again. I wasn't sure why. Chumana had spoken to me normally, not even through my mind. It had all been out loud. Maybe I needed to practice with Brenyx.

"Hey, Brenyx. Can you say 'da'?"

"Da?" Gabe laughed. "Why would you start with that?"

"Well, don't most babies start out saying 'dada'? Maybe it'd be an easier noise for a dragon too."

Gabe shook his head and smiled. Brenyx scampered away to sit a couple of feet from Gabe as he tried to make a fire with his flint stone. She cocked her head as she watched the sparks. Gabe looked at her and chuckled.

"It's called a flint stone. It creates sparks that can then start a fire. Just wait for a moment, and I'll show you," Gabe said.

He leaned down to gently blow on a spark as soon as it touched the bit of dry grass he had added to the top of the pile.

The flame started out small, then it sped up as it reached the dry sticks.

Brenyx purred and sat right next to the flame. She was just about in it, but I didn't say anything. I figured she was a dragon, and their whole world was flame. *Though...*

"Brenyx, please mind your wings. I don't know if those are fireproof."

Brenyx looked at me and spread her wings.

"It's amazing how she seems to understand everything we say," Gabe said.

"Well, they haven't lived for thousands of years without being some form of intelligent creature."

"True. Are you ready for some food?"

"Yes. I'm famished." I rubbed my belly, unfamiliar with going so long without food. I didn't eat all the time at home, but I wasn't one to turn down food.

Gabe dug around in one of our packs and handed me a bit of bread, cheese, and dried meat. He tried to hand some meat to Brenyx, but she must've still been satisfied from her large mouse because she just shook her head and turned her attention back to the fire.

"Do you think she'll go blind staring at the fire like that?" I asked.

Gabe laughed. "You're like a mother hen. I'm sure she'll know when her eyes need a break."

I didn't say anything, because he was right. But I wanted to keep Brenyx safe until I could deliver her to the adult dragons. Though thinking about that made me nervous too. *What if they were mean or tried to kill her? Would they try to kill a baby? What if Chumana was some type of dragon that these dragons hate? Were there dragon wars within the dragon world?*

"What are you thinking?"

Gabe startled me, but I didn't really want to talk about my

concerns in front of Brenyx. I didn't want to worry her, especially since my fears were unfounded.

"Oh, not much. Just our future and what may lie ahead for both us and Brenyx. You know... when she meets the other dragons and what might happen. I don't recall us reading anything about what happens when humans meet dragons—aside from them trying to kill each other. How do we alert them that we want peace? I highly doubt waving a white flag would mean anything to them."

"Sometimes, I feel like we didn't think this through well enough, but if we'd stayed any longer, we'd have run into trouble with a dragon in town. Could you imagine the mob we'd have faced? We already had one man track us down. How many more would have come after us?"

I sighed. Gabe was remarkable at making me feel better. I hoped I could rely on him for the duration of the trip.

"How about you get some rest? I'll take first watch," Gabe said.

"I won't argue about that. Brenyx, I'll put your bag next to me, so if you want to sleep in it, you're more than welcome."

Brenyx made a little rumble and continued staring at the fire. Gabe and I looked at each other and laughed. She sure loved flames. It would be interesting to see what happened once she developed her own. Though maybe it wouldn't be as fascinating then.

I grabbed my blanket roll from the saddlebags and set up my sleeping area not too far from the fire but also not too close. Then I grabbed Brenyx's bag and set it by my head.

"Wake me if anything happens," I told Gabe.

"Of course. You get some sleep. I'll let you know when it's time to switch watch."

I nodded. "Good night, Brenyx. Good night, Gabe."

I crawled into my blankets and fell asleep almost instantly.

CHAPTER

SIXTEEN

I woke to complete darkness. It took me a moment to remember where I was, and once I realized there should have been a fire, I panicked.

"Gabe? Brenyx?" I whispered into the darkness. I tugged on my boots and rubbed my eyes, hoping that would speed their adjustment to the dark.

The fire was completely out. Not a single ember remained. Both our horses were still tied. I reached into the down bag, and Brenyx wasn't there. Gabe wouldn't have left me. At least I didn't think he would without his horse. And if his horse was still tied, then he couldn't have gone far. *But where is Brenyx?*

A twig snapped, and leaves rustled straight across the ashes from me. I remained perfectly still. Whatever it was could most likely see me, and I couldn't see it. I cursed myself for leaving my crossbow out of arm's reach. Rookie mistake. I had already forgotten my lesson learned from Bella's father—always be within reach of my weapons.

A wolf howled off to my left. It had to be only yards away, judging by its volume. The leaves across from me quit moving

105

as if whatever was there had frozen so the wolf couldn't see it. *Is it prey?* I didn't dare call for Gabe or Brenyx. I still didn't want to move. *Where is Gabe?* He wasn't supposed to leave me. He was supposed to keep watch.

I slowly and quietly rolled onto my hands and knees and crept toward my crossbow, watching my surroundings in case I had to dash up the nearest tree. I had nearly reached my weapon when a growl froze me with my arm outstretched. The wolf was upon me. If I survived, Gabe would never hear the end of leaving me behind.

I peered over my shoulder, and sure enough, there stood a massive gray wolf. His eyes reflected in the moonlight. I could barely see him without a fire, but his white teeth shone as he snarled at me. I only had one chance to get my crossbow, but I hadn't left it cocked, so I would have to use it like a club to beat the wolf off me.

Using all my strength, I leaped forward and grabbed my bow. I fell onto my back and swung the bow in front of me, trying to connect with the wolf I was sure had leaped the same moment I had. Instead of my weapon connecting with the wolf, a black blur slammed into the side of the beast, and they went tumbling head over paws several feet away from me. I stole the moment to grab an arrow and put it into my crossbow. I aimed, ready to fire.

The wolf snarled and tried to get away from the blackness. It finally broke free and ran to the edge of the woods but spun around, snapping, snarling, and ready for an attack. My eyes followed its gaze to what looked like another black wolf. *But why would this black wolf protect me?*

"Sof!" Gabe dropped to his knees by my side, his crossbow ready in his hands. He aimed it at the black wolf, whose back was still to us as it faced off with the gray wolf.

"Wait!" I pushed down his bow so he wouldn't shoot it.

"What? Why?"

"That black wolf is… protecting me." I couldn't tear my eyes from the two wolves squaring off.

"But what if it just wants you for its meal?"

I shook my head and continued watching. The black wolf lunged forward, and the gray wolf fled into the woods. The black wolf was right on its heels, nipping at the gray wolf.

I spun to face Gabe and shoved him. "Why did you leave me?"

"I didn't mean to! I was trying to protect you."

"By leaving me? What sense does that make?" I pushed him again.

"These wolves started to surround us, so I chased them off through the woods, but I lost my way. Wait. Where's Brenyx?"

"You didn't take her with you? She wasn't here when I woke up." I panicked. *What happened to her? Did she try to follow Gabe and get lost?*

"No, I didn't. She was in her bag. I thought she was asleep. I knew that she would protect you, so I didn't want her with me," Gabe said.

We both spread out to search our camp, wolves already a distant memory. I double-checked the bag, just in case, but she wasn't there. I checked my blankets.

Gabe got the fire going again, which helped us see. Still no sign of her.

Forgetting about wolves nearby, I gripped my bow tight and called, "Brenyx!"

We both stood still, listening to the woods around us. Plenty of animal sounds filled the night, but no little purr from Brenyx.

"Brenyx!" Gabe and I called together.

Tears warmed my eyes, and I turned my back to Gabe. I

wiped my face and took a deep breath. We just had to wait for daylight, then we could look for tracks.

Gabe's hand squeezed my shoulder, then he let go. "I'm really sorry, Sof. I didn't mean to let you down. I thought for sure she'd stay with you since she was so protective. I never should've run after the wolves."

I shook my head and sniffled. "It's okay, Gabe. We'll find her. We just have to wait until morning. Then we'll track her. I'm sure dragon prints look a lot different than the other critter prints in these woods. And you're right. You shouldn't have chased after those wolves. That's how they trick you to separate you and kill you. So please never chase after anything again. You stay with me, and we'll protect each other." I turned to Gabe.

He nodded and looked at the ground, his eyebrows drawn and his face crumpled. "I promise to never leave your side unless you tell me to."

"Deal."

I stuck out my hand, and we shook on it.

"You get some rest. I'll keep watch and wake you at sunrise. I don't think it'll be much longer now."

"Okay. I am sorry, Sof." Gabe's voice cracked.

"Quit. I know you're sorry. Let's just learn and move on."

He smiled half-heartedly and went to my sleeping area to stretch out on the blankets. I heard a rustle in the brush where the wolves had disappeared to.

"Gabe," I whispered.

We both held our bows prepped and ready where the noise had come from.

A purr mixed with a hint of a growl surprised me.

"Brenyx?" I called.

The black wolf came forward and swished its tail, not quite wagging it.

"Do you think...?" Gabe started but stopped as the wolf shook like it was covered in water.

The black wolf shrank as it shook, and its fur became scales. Then little Brenyx stood before us.

"Oh, Brenyx!" I dropped my crossbow, rushed to her, and fell to my knees.

She leaped up onto my chest, and I squeezed her so tight she grunted.

"I was so worried about you! How did you do that? Oh, I'm so glad you're safe!"

Gabe knelt beside us. Brenyx looked up at him and purred.

"I'm glad to see you, too, kid. You really had us scared."

Brenyx nuzzled my neck again.

As the panic seeped out of my body, I turned to Gabe. His eyes had teared up, but I wouldn't point it out.

"Did you know that dragons could shapeshift?" I asked.

"No, but we definitely know now. I think we'll learn a lot in the next few days."

Brenyx seemed to be more my protector than I was hers. She never let me out of her sight. I still wished she could talk. That would have made everything easier. We packed our belongings and set out. I missed Oliver and wished he were with us. Gabe, Brenyx, and I formed quite the odd little trio.

The farther we traveled, the more overgrown the road became.

"I thought this road was bad to begin with," I said as our horses nearly touched while avoiding the forest overtaking the road.

"Yeah, I think we'll have to go single file here pretty soon.

I'm sure our horses won't appreciate bumping into each other on one side and getting scratched on the other."

Brenyx kept a watchful eye on our surroundings. I wondered just how well she could hear and see. *We read that dragons have amazing eyesight, but are they born with it? Does it get better with age? Do they see by detecting heat, or do they see like humans?* When she was able to talk, I would ask her all my questions.

Gabe pulled his horse to a stop, so I stopped mine as well.

"What is it?" I asked.

"I think you and Brenyx should go ahead. I'll follow and keep an eye on you two," Gabe said.

"You're just afraid I'll shoot you with my bow if something tries to get you." I smirked.

"Well, that too." Gabe laughed.

I laughed, and Brenyx cocked her head while looking at my mouth. *Silly dragon.*

"You have to admit that was funny, Brenyx," Gabe said.

Brenyx looked at him then back at my face. She rumbled a little purr and sat back on my shoulder, watching around us.

"She really is like a guard dog," I said.

"Too bad she isn't bigger," Gabe said.

"I wonder if she could be, though. That wolf she turned into was quite large. Maybe, when she's bigger, she'll be able to shrink too. Just imagine if she could! Do you have any idea how many animals running around could secretly be dragons? Maybe they didn't disappear at all and are living among us."

"Now, that would be something. I don't imagine they could stay that way for long, though. I'd think they'd get stuck or maybe go insane not being in their true form," Gabe said.

"Well, when we meet the dragons, you can ask one."

"If they don't eat us first."

"Hey! Positive thinking. Everything will be okay... I hope.

Now come on, we're burning daylight. You're staying behind us to keep watch then?"

"Yes. I think it'll be safer that way. Brenyx can scout ahead with her dragon senses, and I can watch our backs while I keep an eye on you two."

"Fine. You play chaperone. Us girls will be the bait." I grinned as he searched for words.

"Now, that's just not fair."

I nudged my horse forward and turned to look at him. His mouth kept moving like a fish out of water.

I laughed. "I couldn't help it. You set yourself up for that."

He laughed, and I turned to continue forward.

The trail became single-horse sized only about a mile later. My horse, thankfully, didn't seem too irritated when the brush started rubbing against his sides. The trees rose so high that they blocked most of the light. It chilled me to be in the shade for most of the trip, minus midday. Brenyx didn't seem to mind at all. To my surprise, she stayed quite warm, but perhaps her fire was beginning to grow inside her.

I turned around every now and again to make sure Gabe remained attentive. He smiled at me every time. I flushed the last time and decided I'd better quit looking for a while.

Brenyx studied me curiously and chittered.

"Oh, hush, you. Besides, when are you going to talk? You started to. Do you care to try again?"

Brenyx's reply was complete silence. Not even a purr.

"Okay. Whenever you're ready, then, you just let me know. I won't push you. Are you hungry yet? You haven't scrambled after any rats lately."

Brenyx continued to stare at me.

"Silence it is."

We rode on for a few more hours, until the sky appeared to be nearing dusk.

"I think we should find a place to stop," Gabe said.

I pulled my horse's reins and turned to face Gabe. "How can we find a camp with this overgrown road? I can't even see a place to put the horses before the next bend, which isn't far. Then I think we're almost to the base of the first mountain. You can see it above the trees." I pointed toward what I thought to be north and the peak of a mountain in the distance when I looked straight between the opening in the trees.

Gabe looked around. "Let me try to get through some brush. I'll see if I can find a place to squeeze the horses through."

Gabe dismounted then brought his horse's reins up for me to hold. I decided to dismount and stretch awhile. Sitting all day in the saddle had begun to take a toll on my legs, back, and arms. I hadn't realized until that moment how much my muscles ached. Gabe squeezed past my horse and walked up the trail. He went around the corner and laughed.

Brenyx and I exchanged a confused glance then looked back up the trail where Gabe had disappeared. Curiosity got the best of me, so I led the horses toward him.

He came around the corner. "You're not going to believe this. You have to come and see."

I pulled the horses a little faster, and as I reached the corner, I couldn't help but laugh too. The trees thinned, and just beyond the corner stood a perfect place where we could tie off the horses and camp. It was well off the road but easy to see. Not ideal if we were trying to hide, but so far, we hadn't seen a sign of anybody else on the trail.

"Well done finding us a place to camp," I said.

Gabe chuckled and took his horse's reins from me. "Yeah, I'm pretty sure this will do for tonight."

I smiled then followed as he led us to a nice limb to tie up our horses.

"I'll go see if I can find anything to hunt. Will you and Brenyx be okay so close to the road?" Gabe asked.

I smiled and side-eyed Brenyx on my shoulder.

"I'm pretty sure my guard dragon and I will be fine. If not, you'll hear a shrill scream."

"Okay. As long as you think you'll be okay." Gabe squeezed my shoulder then grabbed his crossbow and stepped gingerly back into the woods.

SEVENTEEN

The next morning, with bellies full, as Gabe had cooked a couple of rabbits for us, we packed our things. Brenyx sat on my horse's back and watched as we gathered everything.

I rolled my sleeping blanket and attached it to my horse's saddle then stood in front of the little dragon. "So, Brenyx, are you ready to find some family members? We get to start our climb up the mountain today."

Brenyx spun in a little circle and purred.

"Well, I'm glad to see she's excited to meet some other dragons," Gabe said.

I giggled. She was so adorable.

"I hope they're excited to meet us as well. We could be eaten by the end of the day, you know." I winked at Gabe.

Gabe shook his head. "Everything will turn out as it should. I have faith that all will be okay."

I took a deep breath and sighed. "I sure hope you're right."

"Of course I'm right." Gabe walked up and bumped my shoulder with his.

I grinned at him then turned my attention back to the little dragon. I put my hand out. "Come on, Brenyx. I need to saddle the horse, please."

Without hesitation, she ran up my arm and perched on my shoulder, wrapping her tail around my neck. Gabe helped me saddle my horse, then he saddled his own. We cleaned up our little camp, and I made sure we hadn't left anything behind as Gabe kicked dirt over our fire.

I untethered my horse from the limb then swung into the saddle, my muscles protesting every movement. Brenyx ran down my arm and up my horse's neck to sit atop his head. I laughed at the absurdity of the little creature, but I found myself falling in love with her—the way she cocked her head as I spoke to her and her big green eyes focusing on my mouth with every word. The intelligence behind her eyes was amazing for just being days old. I marveled at how smart adult dragons must be.

"Do you remember if any of our books said how long dragons live?" I asked as Gabe mounted his horse.

He pursed his lips to the side and drew his eyebrows together. "Honestly, I can't remember anything besides vague references. I know some said hundreds of years, but who knows since humans don't live that long? Unless a dragon told them, I suppose, before they killed each other."

"Hm. I was just thinking about how intelligent Brenyx is already, and she's just barely born. I'm curious how smart these dragons are that we're about to meet."

"Hard to say."

We nudged our horses forward and got back onto the trail, which was, thankfully, much wider. I was confused. The trail appeared to go along the bottom of the mountain for as far as I could see but not up.

"Hey, Gabe? Aren't we going up the north mountains? The trail doesn't appear to."

Gabe pulled his horse next to mine, and he looked at the trail. Our horses plodded along, dutifully following the path.

"I imagine that once the dragons took over this area, not many people wanted to go that direction. Besides, I'm not sure anybody really knows what's over the mountains. So they probably stuck to the lower trail, keeping an eye on the sky. I think we'll have to forge a path up that won't be too steep for our horses," Gabe said.

I nodded and looked at the mountains. Considering how steep and forested they appeared, I suspected we would have a hard time finding an easy path. The base of the mountains was covered in a lot of rocks, all the way from pebbles to massive boulders. So many rocks littered the space that the trees couldn't grow well at the base of the mountains, but they did grow thicker as the mountain rose.

"How far do you think we should travel before we try to head up?" I asked.

"I think as soon as we see a spot we can take, we should go for it. I don't recall a specific place north of the mountains where dragons might be, so I think we'd better try when we can. Just keep your eyes open, and if you see a spot you think we should try, let me know. I'll do the same."

"Okay. Brenyx, help us find a spot where we can start climbing, okay?"

Brenyx looked at me, cocking her head to the side as usual. She purred and swished her tail then turned back to watch our path ahead. It made me wonder what she was searching for. She had been looking north for most of our travels, with the exception of glancing around every now and then. *Does she understand that we're searching for other dragons?* I wondered if we would have some way of knowing if they were family. *Do dragons have families?* So many questions. Hopefully, I would learn the answers before I was eaten.

We traveled along the base of the mountain for a couple of hours. I felt nervous, thinking that maybe we would never find a good place to lead the horses. Brenyx looked toward the top of the mountains almost nonstop. She would turn and look at me every now and then, almost as if to ask when we would head that way.

"Gabe, do you think we've missed our opportunity to head north?"

Gabe sighed. His eyes searched my face. "I'm beginning to worry that we should've gone the other way."

Maybe we were supposed to go west. "But I don't think the trail led that way. That's why we came east."

"But what if there was a lesser-traveled road that would take us north? Then we've been going the wrong way for hours. Maybe we should turn around and try it. But then we lose an entire morning. What do you think?" Gabe asked.

Brenyx turned to face us when we talked. She stared intently at me.

"Brenyx, what do you think we should do? Should we turn back? Should we keep trudging forward and hope that we didn't make a horrible mistake? Where do we go? We want to get up the mountain, but we need terrain that the horses can manage, and so far, it looks too steep."

Brenyx continued to stare at me, and I wasn't sure if she expected me to keep talking or if she was thinking. Gabe shrugged. We both looked back at Brenyx, who had turned her attention to the mountains. Brenyx sniffed the air, bobbing her head up and down then left to right. She closed her eyes and took one large inhale. Her tail swished side to side in slow motion. Her eyes popped open, and she chittered at me.

"I don't know what you're saying, Brenyx," I told her.

Brenyx grunted and scurried down my horse's leg. My horse jerked to the side at the sensation, but I held the reins tight.

"Brenyx! Where are you going?"

Brenyx scurried up the road in the direction we had been heading.

Gabe shrugged. "Might as well follow her."

I nodded and nudged my horse forward. Brenyx's little black form looked like a snake slithering down the road as she weaved along the dirt and gravel. She would drop her nose to the ground then stop and look around. She inclined her head as she regarded the mountain looming over us. The thick trees made it seem impossible to find a good place to ascend. Brenyx grunted and stared at me.

"Did you find it? Is this where we go up?" I asked her.

Brenyx purred and slithered north. I urged my horse to pick up the speed so we didn't lose her. When I turned, Gabe was right behind me. Brenyx paused periodically to look back at us. She wove through the trees, finding large enough spaces that our horses had no trouble following her. She also had us zigzagging east and west as we went north.

Despite the mountains appearing too steep for our horses, Brenyx's path made it remarkably easy. I wondered if she could communicate with or sense other dragons and that was how she knew where to go. I turned as well as I could in my saddle to look at Gabe.

"How do you think she knows where we're going? She's an infant," I said.

"Well, all birds know to fly south for the winter. Maybe this is her flight south?"

"Hm. I never thought of it like that. So we think it's her instincts. Hopefully, they help her find nice dragons."

Gabe laughed. "Nice dragons, huh? I don't know if such a thing exists."

"But there must be. All those books on dragons couldn't have been written about dragons that killed humans the moment they saw them. I mean, yes, some dragons were mean. But were they mean because humans wanted to kill every dragon they saw without trying to communicate with them? Chumana was nice. And do you think Brenyx will be able to save us if they are mean dragons? Will they listen to a brand-new dragon? Or is it like that thing where you have to listen to your parents and elders, and they won't listen to you even if you might be right?"

"Wow. Does your brain ever stop?" Gabe asked.

I rolled my eyes. "No. Unfortunately, it does not. It's why I have trouble sleeping at night. At least I did before this journey."

The forest seemed to grow dimmer, and the trees' shadows stretched along the ground.

"Um. It's getting kind of dark. Do you think we should stop?"

Gabe called, "Hey, Brenyx! It's getting dark. We need to set up camp."

Brenyx stopped where she was and turned to look at Gabe and me in turn. She looked back toward the top of the mountain. I could almost hear the sigh she released as her little wings slumped, and she tromped back to our horses. If she could have spoken, I was sure I would've heard her give a grudging "fine." I couldn't help smiling, but I didn't dare laugh. I knew we were close, and she must feel it. I still couldn't shake my fear. We could all die soon. The dragons could take one look at us, see that we were human, and poof, gone in a flash of fire and ash.

"Hey."

I turned to Gabe, his eyebrows drawn in with concern.

"I'm okay," I lied. "Just thinking of tomorrow."

"Everything will be all right. I can feel it. Besides, do you honestly think Brenyx will let them hurt us—well, you? I'm still questionable."

Gabe grinned, and I couldn't help but giggle.

Brenyx looked up at us, obviously annoyed that we were happy about stopping.

"I'm sorry, Brenyx. We should be there soon. But let's arrive fully rested. Now, let's make camp."

EIGHTEEN

The next morning, my body felt cold and stiff. I realized I was frozen in fear. All I'd wanted before was to keep Brenyx safe because I had promised her mother. But suddenly, I wondered if I should tell her to head north without me. We had made it close enough. Brenyx could make it the rest of the way on her own. *Right?*

As if she'd heard my thoughts, Brenyx scampered onto my chest. She sat and put her nose so close, I could smell the smoked meat on her breath. She then closed her eyes and held her snout to mine. I sighed.

"Thank you, Brenyx. I needed that."

Brenyx purred and did one complete circle. She twitched her tail then ran into the woods, presumably for her breakfast. Gabe was getting the horses ready.

"Hey, you should've woken me up." I climbed out of my blankets and began rolling them.

"I figured you needed your rest." Gabe walked over, took my roll, and packed it onto my horse, then he scuffed some dirt over the fire.

"Well, thank you. I'm not sure I slept much, though. Gabe, I'm honestly scared. We could be dead later today."

"Or... we could become friends with another dragon."

I smiled. *Always so positive.*

"There it is." He stepped close and pulled me into a hug. "No matter what happens, just know that I can die a happy man after having this adventure with you."

I squeezed him back, heat rushing through my body, then stepped away. "Thank you, Gabe. For everything."

He nodded, and we both finished packing. I ate a little bit while waiting for Brenyx to return. Shortly after I finished, she came trotting out of the woods, licking her lips. Whatever she'd had must've been okay raw. As far as I knew, she still didn't have her flame.

"You ready, Brenyx?" I asked.

Her tail shot into the air, and she danced from foot to foot.

"I take that as a yes." Gabe grinned.

"Okay. Let's get going. Ready to lead the way again, Brenyx?" I asked.

Brenyx looked northward then began scouting out the terrain.

As we climbed the mountain, the trees thinned. I could see at least fifty feet in each direction and felt exposed. I saw no good places to run or hide our horses. There weren't even shrubs growing that high up, just a few scattered trees here and there, revealing the peak of the mountain between their leaves. I glanced skyward, half expecting to see the shape of a dragon overhead. Gabe seemed just as uncomfortable as I felt, glancing to the sky about every ten seconds and shifting in his saddle. He looked my way, and I kept my eyes forward.

"It's okay. I'm nervous too," Gabe said.

I released a whoosh of air.

"I think I'm more than nervous. I'm terrified. We're almost

to the peak, and Brenyx seems to be impatient for us to keep up. Did you notice how she looks over her shoulder all the time now?"

Gabe nodded. "I did. But I wondered if she's just being protective of you. You saw how she behaved with those wolves."

"Do you really think she'll protect me against her own kind? Isn't that... unnatural?"

Gabe considered me a moment. "I guess we'll have to wait and see."

I sighed. "I guess so."

We continued onward and upward until the trees were almost nonexistent. Only a handful of trees stood in any direction, and I saw no trees at all toward the top of the mountain. *Where could dragons possibly hide?*

The terrain grew so rocky that our horses stumbled more than walked. Brenyx slowed and looked over her shoulder at us even more often than before. I wasn't sure if it was nerves or if she was waiting for our horses. Maybe Gabe was right that she was being protective. We probably only had about two hundred feet to reach the peak.

"I think we should stop for a moment," I said.

Brenyx turned and inclined her head.

Gabe practically mirrored the movement. "Why?"

"I'd like to gather my belongings from the horses. They're struggling enough as it is, and when a dragon appears, they'll be terrified and bolt. I'd like to have some of my food and supplies before they run off. I'd also rather not be thrown onto this rocky surface."

Gabe chewed the inside of his lip then inclined his head. "That makes sense. These are my father's horses, though, so I hope he'll forgive me for losing them."

"If you come home alive after meeting dragons, I'm sure you'll be forgiven," I said.

He smirked. "You do have a point. This will be a remarkable story. Hopefully, he believes it."

"Yes. That too."

We dismounted and grabbed our packs. Brenyx supervised the whole time, simultaneously watching all around us, including looks toward the sky and the top of the mountain. We removed the saddles and bridles from the horses so they wouldn't get caught on anything during their journey back down the mountain.

I patted my horse's neck. "Thank you for bringing us this far. You should head back home because this could get pretty scary. You just stay safe."

I kissed my horse's nose, and he nickered at me. We stared at each other for a few seconds more, then he nickered to the other horse, and they walked away down the mountain.

"Ready?" Gabe asked.

"Ready. I think."

Brenyx waited until we began walking north before she started scouting. It was nearly dusk, and I really wished we had more trees for cover. *Can dragons see in the dark?* They had to be able to. I readjusted my packs on my shoulders and kept my eyes on the sky.

We were nearly to the peak when Brenyx froze. Gabe swung his arm in front of me, stopping me from going farther. We quickly looked at each other then back at Brenyx. She'd assumed a startled-cat posture, her back arched and her spikes standing straight. She was about twenty feet in front of us, but I swore she growled. My heart pounded in my ears, and I felt dizzy. That was it. *But where is one?*

"Who dares upon the dragons' territory?" a gravelly, earth-shaking voice bellowed.

I couldn't breathe. My legs quivered. Gabe's hand gripped my arm. I turned to him, and his eyes went wide, his only outward sign of fear.

"I—we are here with Chumana's daughter!" I yelled toward the peak.

The ground beneath my feet shook, and rocks tumbled down the mountain. Brenyx ran toward me, whipped around when she reached my feet, and spread her wings. If I hadn't been so terrified, the look of her defiance against an unseen dragon would've made me laugh. I appreciated her attempt to protect me, even if she couldn't.

"How do you know of Chumana? Did you murder her, as your kind murders all dragons they come across?"

I resisted covering my ears to protect them from his booming voice. The rocks at the peak split, and a gray dragon, larger than Chumana, blasted rocks every which way as it flung open its wings. Gabe wrapped me in his arms, tucking my head into his chest. When the rocks settled, we both turned, and I gasped at the dragon in front of us. Its eyes blazed red, and tears streaked its wings. Its tail lashed back and forth. It took one step forward, and I nearly lost my balance.

Brenyx gave the tiniest roar compared to the massive beast that towered over us. I dared to look back at the dragon's face. Amazingly enough, the dragon tilted its head and raised its brows.

"Who is this youngling?" the dragon asked.

"This is the child of Chumana!" Gabe yelled.

The dragon stepped back, and Gabe and I held onto each other for balance.

"You have said Chumana's name twice. How did you learn it before you killed her?" The dragon's voice, while still loud, didn't sound as threatening as it had just moments before.

"We didn't kill her. She came to me... dying. She was trying to find a place for her egg, and dragon hunters had speared her out of the sky. I don't know how long she flew, but she wound up in my backyard. She asked me to make sure that her egg hatched because she didn't want dragons to go extinct. She didn't give me a lot of information, but from our research, we thought we could bring the egg—well, now, dragon—for you to raise right."

The dragon stood staring at us. I chanced a look at Gabe, and he shrugged one shoulder ever so slightly. Brenyx still stood, wings spread wide, holding her defensive stance in front of us.

The large dragon tucked in its wings and lowered itself to the ground. "What is your name, little one?"

Brenyx roared with all her might yet was still quiet compared to the larger dragon. I wasn't sure whether I would hear human words or if she would just sound like a dragon. She tried to make herself larger, stretching her wings so far, I feared her shoulder bones would break.

"She says her name is Brenyx. Did you name her?" the dragon asked, his voice less earthshaking that time.

"We did, but we asked her what she thought first," I said.

The dragon considered that a moment. "Brenyx, I will not hurt you or your friends. But you all must go before the dragon council so we can decide what to do with you."

Brenyx growled.

"What to do with us? Like kill us or let us go?" Gabe asked.

"Not many humans dare come here anymore, except the most obsessive hunters. They are easy to spot, and we kill them instantly. You three, however, are odd. I can sense and see a deep loyalty between you and Brenyx. It is unusual for a dragon to bond so quickly. This deserves attention much greater than mine. You have my word that no harm will come to you before you speak to the council," the dragon said.

Gabe shrugged and held out his palms as if to say, *What choice do we have?* I wanted them to take care of Brenyx, but I needed to make sure they would before I left her with strange dragons.

"My only concern is that Brenyx is taken care of. I want your word that no matter what becomes of Gabe and me, you will ensure Brenyx is brought up right," I said.

The dragon chuckled. "What do you humans think of us? We aren't murderous beasts. Of course we will take care of her. Now, come along. My replacement should be here shortly, as it's nearly night, then I will take you the rest of the way. What do you call yourselves?"

Brenyx tucked her wings against her sides. Her tail slowly swished side to side. I took it as a good sign.

"My name is Sofia—"

"Daughter of Wisdom."

"Yes. That's what Chumana said to me too. And this is Gabriel."

Gabe inclined his head in greeting.

"Interesting. Strength and Wisdom," the dragon said.

"And what do you call yourself?" I asked.

"You may call me Dereus." He turned and looked behind him. "And my replacement is here."

Another gray dragon, not quite as massive as Dereus, landed next to him.

"Dereus," the dragon said.

"Kona. These here need to go to the council. They are the only thing that happened today. Nothing else to report. No movement in any direction."

Kona turned to face us. Standing in the presence of two

large dragons was even more intimidating, though Kona didn't have the earthshaking voice Dereus did.

"And who is the little one?" Kona asked.

"That is Brenyx. They say she is the daughter of Chumana." Dereus's tone told me he didn't quite believe us.

"Chumana?" Kona whispered almost breathlessly. He lowered himself and put his chin on the ground. "Brenyx, if your mother was truly Chumana, it is an honor to meet you, Your—"

"Enough. We will find out if what they say is true," Dereus said.

"Yes, sir." Kona pulled himself back upright.

"Now, let's get you camouflaged."

Kona wriggled down into the stones, and Dereus pushed more atop him. I had wondered how Dereus could hide himself like that. Once Kona blended in, I could barely tell he wasn't a pile of rocks. The two dragons exchanged a few words that they kept to themselves. A remarkable feat, considering how loud they had been before. Dereus nodded at Kona then turned toward us.

"All right, you three. Are you ready to meet the council?"

"I think so," I said.

"Okay, then I will have you all ride at the base of my neck. It would take too long for you to walk. So climb on." Dereus laid his neck on the ground.

Gabe's smile seemed more excited than scared to me. I reached down, and Brenyx scurried up my arm and perched on my shoulder with her tail around my neck. Gabe offered me his hand, and I held it as I put my other hand on Dereus's neck. It was remarkably smooth and almost metallic. His scales felt cool, just like Chumana's.

I climbed atop his neck, then Gabe hopped on after me.

"Hold on tight. Liftoff is a bit abrupt," Dereus said as Gabe grabbed my waist, Brenyx wrapped her tail tighter around my neck, and I squeezed one of the spikes in front of me.

As the air was sucked from my lungs, we were off toward the evening sky.

NINETEEN

After getting past my terror of being so high in the air that I could barely make out the shapes below us, I realized how exhilarating it felt to be free. Dereus gave us a smooth flight. I feared that I would need a death grip on his spike the whole time we were in the air, but since he didn't jerk about, I actually let go. None of us spoke or even tried. We just took in the world far below us.

Brenyx seemed thrilled to be up in the air. She still held onto my neck with her tail, but her little body bobbed like she was learning how to fly from watching Dereus. I couldn't help but smile at the little beast. I was sad knowing that my time with her would come to an end. Whether by our deaths or from leaving her with the dragons so Gabe and I could head home, I knew I would have to say goodbye soon.

"Hold on back there," Dereus said.

Gabe wrapped an arm around my waist while I grabbed onto Dereus's spike again. As Dereus dove, I thought we might crash into the earth. My stomach lurched into my throat, and I felt lightheaded. I closed my eyes and focused on not losing my grip. Dereus flattened himself out, and I slammed back into Gabe, knocking the breath out of him.

"Sorry!" I yelled, hoping I was loud enough to be heard over the air whooshing around us.

"I'm okay," Gabe said into my ear and squeezed my waist.

Brenyx purred and looked at me sideways.

"We're just about there," Dereus said.

I looked around us since the ground was close enough that I could make things out again. We flew straight toward a bunch of cave openings in the side of a huge rock mountain.

"Cover your ears," Dereus said.

I released his spike to obey, and Gabe let go of me.

Dereus roared one long tone then two shorter ones. His roar vibrated through my entire body, rattling my teeth against each other.

Dereus aimed us toward the largest cavern. I supposed the holes in the mountain wall had to be big enough for the expanse of each dragon's wings. I wondered how Dereus would compare to other dragons. *Would he be smaller? Larger? Average?*

"Don't worry, humans. You have come in peace. The council just needs to speak to you," Dereus said as he evened out and landed smoothly on the edge of the cavern.

He walked about fifty feet then lay down. I took that as my cue to get down. I watched Gabe slide down Dereus's side. He stumbled, but Dereus was quick to put his wing behind Gabe until he stood straight.

"Wow. I didn't realize how shaky my legs would be." Once Gabe was stable, he walked over to me and lifted his arms. "Come on. I've got you."

I leaned over and put my hands on his shoulders. He grabbed my waist and lifted me down so I wouldn't fall. Brenyx kept her tail tight around my neck. Gabe held onto me for a moment until I took a few steps forward. My legs were shaky but not so bad that I couldn't stand on my own.

Dereus tucked in his wings and stood. "Let's get moving. My call will have alerted all who need to come for a meeting of the council. It'd be best if we weren't standing on the ledge as they all arrive," Dereus said.

"Is it dark in there?" Not that I was afraid of the dark, but I was afraid of the dark filled with dragons.

"No, child. We have the light of our fire."

I sighed. At least we wouldn't get ambushed. Gabe and I walked next to Dereus, hurrying to keep up with each step he took. Thankfully, he was right about their fire lighting the way. Extra-large torches that resembled human ones lit the way along every path we followed, keeping the shadows away.

"Are you nervous?" Gabe whispered to me.

"A little. This could be the end of us. I know they won't kill Brenyx, but who knows what they will do to two puny humans? Are you nervous?" I asked.

"A little." Gabe smiled. "But if these are our last moments together, just know that I am really glad I met you."

I stumbled, and Gabe caught my arm, keeping me upright. "You are? Even though I'm leading you to your possible death?"

"I wouldn't want to die with anybody else."

I flushed. Brenyx purred and rubbed her head against my cheek.

"I—"

"We're here," Dereus said.

Gabe and I looked ahead, and I was grateful Dereus had stopped us. We stood in front of an enormous crater within the mountain. It was ridged with ledges that circled around and around, almost like a theater for dragons. A larger ledge in the center of one side had the perfect view of the entire crater. That must have been where the council sat. A raised rock formation with a smooth top stood in the crater's center. That must have been where Gabe and I would find ourselves shortly.

"We will wait over there until the council calls us." Dereus swung his head toward an area off to the side.

It had to be some form of dragon waiting area. The shallow cutout in the wall wasn't so deep that it could qualify as another cave. The opening faced the crater.

He led us over, and I sat on the ground. Gabe sat next to me. Brenyx chose to stay atop my shoulder. I was surprised that she hadn't scampered down to look around yet. Maybe she figured she had time to do so later. Or maybe she was just as nervous as we were but didn't want to let on.

"I meant it," Gabe said.

I flushed again and cleared my throat. "I know you did. I wouldn't want to die with anybody else, either. Thank you for all your help. Even when I tried to drive you away in the very beginning, you stayed."

"You two speak as though you're at your end. I don't think it will come to that. You don't seem like harmful creatures. Though I cannot speak for the council if they will believe your existence is a threat. You now know where we live," Dereus said.

"Well, that doesn't make much sense. Everybody knows where you live. Ask any human, and they will say the north mountains. We just did some extra research trying to understand you. We didn't learn a whole lot. It doesn't seem as though humans and dragons are meant to be friends," I said.

"We were friends once… ages ago, it feels. Then everyone began killing each other. Each side has its own story, but all I saw was blood and murder. I won't harm anyone unless they try to harm me or mine. If that was how we all got along, there wouldn't be so many feuds and hate. But we fear now that humans want to end us all. Is it the same for humans?"

"Yes, pretty much. We were so fearful of Brenyx hatching when we were around others. We were lucky she hatched on the road. However, my brother had to turn back after he got shot by a dragon hunter. The hunter's daughter worked for Gabe's father, and when she told her father of Brenyx, he followed us onto the trail. My brother took an arrow to his leg. Otherwise, he would be with us as well," I said.

"That is unfortunate. Your brother, will he be okay? And what of the dragon hunter?" Dereus asked.

"My brother should be okay as long as no infection sets in. And the dragon hunter is no longer in this world," I said.

"I hate to say good, but I'm glad one less dragon hunter roams the earth." Dereus turned his attention back to the crater. "Look, child. Dragons are arriving."

I didn't want to hang over the edge, but I inched close enough to get a glimpse. I gasped. The dragons were beautiful. They came in every color imaginable. The size difference between them shocked me. Some were no bigger than a sheep, and others were even larger than Dereus. Dozens had already arrived and found a place to settle.

I turned to Dereus. "Are the smaller ones young? Or are some dragons smaller than others?"

Dereus watched the crowd of incoming dragons. "The answer is complicated. Yes, some are younger, so they will be smaller, but some are smaller depending upon their lineage. Those under one hundred years old will not be their full size, as they are still younglings—"

"One hundred? How long do dragons live?" Gabe's eyes bugged.

I couldn't help but giggle despite being just as shocked.

Dereus rumbled a chuckle. "If we lead a healthy life, we can live around twelve hundred years. We are considered adults, as you humans understand it, once we reach one hundred years old. We become respectable elders once we reach eight hundred." Dereus scanned the dragons. "Most of them have arrived. As soon as the council convenes, I will fly you down to the platform."

"Will you stay with us?" I rubbed my chest, trying to calm my anxiety.

Gabe stepped up next to me and clasped my shoulder. I half smiled. I appreciated his support, but I didn't think anything could completely calm me. Brenyx gently squeezed my neck with her tail. I would really miss her.

"I can only deliver you to the platform. I will be just behind you, though, in that seating past the platform. It is for those associated with the people being questioned," Dereus said.

A roar shook the ground, and I backed away from the ledge.

"That means they're ready for you. Are you three ready?" Dereus asked.

Gabe's eyes darted around. I reached out and grabbed his hand. His eyes met mine, and I smiled.

"We're ready," I said.

"All right. Then climb aboard, and I'll take you down. There is nothing to fear. The council is experienced in all situations. And Chumana, well, she was very special to us all. Just be sure to tell every detail, no matter how small it may seem to you. Any questions?"

"Will we live?" Gabe asked.

"I believe you will. Now, climb on." Dereus lay down so we could climb onto his back.

I would have preferred to hear a yes, but his answer was better than a no. I straddled Dereus's neck, then Gabe climbed on after me. He gripped my waist again, and I clutched Dereus's spike. The great dragon spread his wings and sailed down to the platform, spiraling until he landed smoothly and lay down once more.

"I'll be right over there." Dereus gestured with his head toward the area behind us. "You'll be okay. The council is the eldest of us, and they are kind, not quick to anger like some. Just be honest. Dragons hate dishonesty."

All I could do was nod. My mouth had gone dry, and I couldn't look at the hundreds of dragons staring down at us. I felt tiny and insignificant. My thighs shook, and my feet stuck to the ground. Dereus made a small leap and sailed over to his designated spot.

Gabe grabbed my hand. "Come on. Let's go stand in the center and face the council."

I shuffled forward to await our fate.

Three dragons stared down at us from the council seating area. The one in the center was largest and as black as a raven. They were hard to compare, with the council standing several levels up, but the black dragon appeared to be even larger than Dereus. The two other dragons looked slightly smaller but not by much. The one to the right of the black dragon was a beautiful reddish orange. The other was an emerald color. They all kept their wings folded neatly against their sides as they stared down at us. I couldn't read any emotion on their faces.

The murmur of the dragons in the crater sounded like a swarm of bees. Gabe squeezed my hand encouragingly. Beads of sweat appeared along his hairline and on the tip of his nose. He looked sideways at me but didn't face me. I took that as maybe I shouldn't be looking at him either. Brenyx rubbed her cheek against mine and purred. I leaned into her for what could be one of the last times.

"Silence!" the black dragon roared, and the crowd immediately hushed.

Not one voice lingered in the air.

"My name is Baltasar," the black dragon said in a deep, rumbly male voice. "I am one of three council members. To my right is Sule, and to my left is Galik. We are equals on this council, and all decisions must be unanimous. We need to know what brought you here and how you came by your dragon companion. If you lie, we will know. Lying brings certain death. Truth, no matter how painful, must be told. You are the first humans to come into this lair in many years. The last before you were the ones who started the war when they wanted to kill us all. I hope that this will not be the second dragon–human war. Now, children, you may start with what you call yourselves, as you now know who we are, but we've yet to meet you."

I cleared my throat and gripped Gabe's hand tighter. "Hello, council. Thank you for having us here. My name is Sofia, and this is my partner, Gabriel. This dragon is Brenyx. She is the child of Chumana."

The dragons roared, and I flinched, pushing closer to Gabe's side. Brenyx looked at the dragons around us and bared her teeth. Gabe leaned into me just as much as I did him.

"Silence!" Baltasar called, and again, the cavern fell silent immediately.

I dared to look at the council, and the three dragons exchanged looks but no words.

"Daughter of Wisdom, do you know who Chumana is to us?" Sule asked in a voice that sounded much like Chumana's.

Realizing that Sule meant me, I answered, "No, ma'am. She only told me to take care of her egg and make sure that it hatched. She asked me to make sure her child was raised well and told me dragons are being hunted to extinction. She was trying to find a safe place to raise her baby when she was attacked by a dragon hunter. She landed... or crashed... in my yard. Her only concern was her egg and making sure dragons didn't go extinct. She never mentioned where she came from. We only found this place from reading old accounts of dragons and hoping we went in the right direction. Brenyx helped lead us up the mountain."

The dragons exchanged another look. Gabe glanced at me and gave a slight shake of his head. I had no idea how to interpret that. I looked back up at the council only to find them staring at us. My heart raced, and it took everything in my power to not rub my chest to calm myself. Brenyx rubbed her cheek against mine, and I leaned my head toward her. She always seemed to know what I needed.

"We need to discuss this situation." Galik had the same rumble of a voice as Baltasar. "You three, stay where you are. Dereus, you can—"

A shriek blasted through the cavern. I covered my ears, but the sound still made my teeth chatter. I dropped to my knees, and Gabe dropped beside me, his hands over his ears. Brenyx rumbled a growl on my shoulder. Her tail released my neck, and her spikes stood straight in the air. Everyone in the cavern stood on alert. The shriek grew louder as whoever it was came closer. I couldn't keep the sound from piercing through my body.

"Fennewick, no! Stop!" Baltasar roared as he spread his wings over Sule and Galik.

A blue streak of a dragon flew out of one of the caverns toward the ceiling and hurtled toward us. The death I had expected had arrived. I leaned toward Gabe, pressing my forehead against his. I wouldn't have even noticed that Brenyx had left my shoulder except Gabe's eyes went wide, and his mouth opened as if to yell. I spun and saw Brenyx leap a few feet in front of us and spread her wings. Bless that little dragon who thought she could hold off the blue dragon on its way to kill us.

Brenyx squealed a roar that could only belong to a baby dragon, but the sound went from a high-pitched shriek to a lion's roar. I gaped at her.

"Brenyx?" I called, but she didn't turn my way.

Her eyes followed the blue dragon at the top of the cavern as it circled, staring at us. The blue dragon turned and dove. Brenyx roared and snapped her jaws. She pumped her wings and shot into the air—something I didn't even know she could do—and a blast of light engulfed her. I squinted, and when my eyes adjusted to the brilliance, Brenyx was no longer a baby. Blue-and-orange flames covered her body, and she rivaled Dereus in size. She hovered in the air above us, facing the blue dragon above.

TWENTY

"Brenyx?"

I couldn't even hear her name leave my mouth over the sound of the dragons in attendance, but Brenyx turned and looked at me then purred. She focused her attention back on the blue dragon above and snarled as she watched it. The blue dragon hovered in midair, watching us.

The general beehive murmur returned among the dragons in the cavern. They each seemed to be talking to whichever dragon was closest. The council stared at Brenyx in what I imagined was disbelief, their eyes wide and mouths open. Baltasar looked up at the blue dragon.

"Fennewick, halt! I command you to stop this immediately!" Baltasar roared as he continued to hold his wings over Sule and Galik.

Fennewick hovered near the top of the cavern. "You command me? How do you know they did not kill Chumana and steal her egg?"

I couldn't help it anymore. I rubbed my chest, trying to calm the anxiety that flooded me and made my legs shake. I breathed in through my nose and out through my mouth as slowly as possible.

"Do you honestly believe these children are capable of that? Their story held no lies, Fennewick. And look at how Brenyx loves them. Even an egg knows when it has been stolen. Do you think she would protect her captors?" Sule asked.

"Fennewick, your offspring is the first dragon in centuries to change her size to protect a human. Do you know what this means of your child?" Baltasar asked in a soothing rumble.

Fennewick's wings lost their rhythm, and he slowly descended. Brenyx lowered herself to the ground, lost the blue-and-orange flames, and backed up so I stood by her back hip. She broke eye contact with Fennewick to look at Gabe and me then inclined her head and purred. She sounded much louder as a full-size dragon. Then she turned her attention back to Fennewick.

Fennewick lowered himself onto a ledge across from us as several other dragons moved and allowed him the space.

He narrowed his eyes at us. "Who was Chumana to you?" Fennewick's voice shook the cavern. A few pebbles fell from the walls.

Brenyx held her ground.

"I met her as she was dying. She told me to take care of her egg and make sure that her baby survived. She feared your extinction from being hunted by humans. I then watched as she turned to ash, and her ashes spiraled toward the heavens. I can't say that she was my friend, because I only knew her for a few minutes, but she seemed incredible." The words tumbled from my mouth so fast that they blended into one long sentence.

Fennewick growled and looked up at the council. "You honestly believe this monster?"

"We do," all three answered at once.

"She does not have an evil bone in her body. Look at how Brenyx protects her. Brenyx, who was a mere wyrmling just a moment ago. Fennewick, you are consumed by your hatred. Chumana was your mate and queen. News of her death hurt every one of us but you most of all. Do not let your hatred blind you to the fact that your offspring is standing in front of you, ready to fight to protect these humans," Baltasar said.

At the word "offspring," Brenyx faltered. She bumped me with her hip as she stumbled then regained her stance against the dragon who must be her father. Her spikes along her back stood straight, and her tail swished from side to side. I risked another glance at Gabe. His eyes went back and forth between Brenyx and Fennewick. He caught me looking at him.

"They said Chumana was queen," Gabe whispered.

The information didn't sink in at first. I just shook my head, then I realized he meant that we'd been taking care of a princess the whole time. *The dragon princess. Royalty.* The hum of the other dragons had stopped. Like Gabe, they continued to look from Fennewick to Brenyx.

"Fennewick, you are not a young dragon anymore. You didn't answer the question. Do you know what it means that Brenyx is standing in front of us full grown?" Galik asked.

Fennewick grumbled. "Yes."

I waited, hoping Fennewick would explain, because I had no idea what was going on. Even the other dragons around us looked at each other, shrugging or shaking their heads. So at least we humans weren't the only ones who didn't know. Gabe stared at me with his mouth open and his eyes wide.

"What?" I whispered.

He shook his head slowly from side to side, his mouth still open.

"Stop it. Close your mouth," I whispered.

He quickly did. We turned and found the council staring at us.

"Son of Strength, you are gaping at your friend as if you have figured out exactly what she is. Would you care to explain it? I see that a lot of our younger dragon brethren do not know the significance of Brenyx's change either," Sule said.

I was strangely comforted by Sule's voice. I didn't know if it was because she seemed motherly to me or because she sounded so much like Chumana.

Gabe nodded. He licked his lips and took a step back from me then scanned the dragons anxiously awaiting his explanation. "Most don't know of the change today because, as Baltasar said earlier, it hasn't happened for centuries. The only reason I know is because, when we were researching how to take care of Chumana's egg, I ran across the information. And just so you all know, Brenyx even changed into a wolf to protect Sofia on the trip here. But it is said that if a baby dragon can shapeshift before its first moon, it is forever linked to a human, whether that human is with the dragon or not."

Gabe brought his eyes to mine, and my mouth went dry. *I'm connected to Brenyx?*

"And what does this mean of the human, Son of Strength?" Baltasar asked.

Gabe took my hands in his. "It means that the human is linked to the dragons. It means that Sofia is a dragoness."

TWENTY-ONE

Roars and speaking filled the entire cavern. The beehive swarmed. Gabe squeezed my hands, and he smiled at me. Not a single dragon stood still. Dereus, who had been remarkably quiet the whole time, stared at me in wonder. I turned to Brenyx. If a dragon could smile, she was doing it. She looked back at Fennewick then turned to face me. She made one bounce and grabbed me in her arms. Wrapping her wings around me, she purred so hard my teeth rattled and I vibrated down to my toes.

"Brenyx, you're squishing me," I breathed.

Brenyx released her grip and set me down. She put her forehead to mine, and I closed my eyes.

"Okay, everyone. Quiet," Baltasar commanded.

That time, it took a little longer for everyone to settle down.

"Son of Strength, thank you for the explanation. Now, for the rest of the story, as I'm sure your human documents don't tell much more than that"—Gabe shook his head—"being connected to each other is one thing. But the connection's purpose is to bring peace to the realm.

"Daughter of Wisdom, you were chosen for this position because you are pure of heart. Chumana was probably drawn to you, and fate would have it that you two met. Chumana was our queen. Brenyx, here, is our princess. As a dragoness, when the ceremony is complete, you will have a difficult life because you will belong neither to the human realm nor the dragon realm. You can choose to not accept this life, for it is not an easy one. You and Brenyx will need to consider your futures because the same goes for her. Being as she will always protect a human, she will be ridiculed among dragons, the same as you will be among humans. We will give you until tomorrow evening to make your decision. Dereus will show you to a cave where you three can sleep for tonight." Baltasar inclined his head toward Dereus. "Everyone is dismissed. Fennewick, if I may have a word, please."

Fennewick looked at us, his gaze lingering on Brenyx. I wondered how he could be anything but ecstatic to see his offspring. Then again, I still didn't know a lot about the ways of dragons. He clearly loved Chumana, though. He launched into the air and landed on the council's ledge. Brenyx watched him go then shook herself down to her normal size. Dereus landed behind me, and I knelt so Brenyx could run up my arm to station herself on my neck.

"You three are amazing. I never thought I'd see another connected pair in my lifetime. It's so rare," Dereus said.

The whole situation made me so uncomfortable that I just kept quiet and smiled. Gabe beamed. He came over and one-armed hugged me, careful not to disturb Brenyx. She bumped her cheek against mine, and relief filled me. I wondered if she felt as out of her body as I did. I couldn't possibly be a drag-oness. My biggest problem in life was supposed to be my mother trying to marry me off. Not bringing peace to the world. But Chumana had called me a dragoness. I just hadn't realized what she had meant when she'd said it. Her death had taken over my thoughts.

"Are you ready?" Dereus asked.

I shook my head to clear it and smiled again. "I'm ready."

Dereus lowered himself to the ground. We climbed onto his back, and Gabe sat behind me again, holding my waist. I grabbed Dereus's spike, and Brenyx wrapped her tail around my neck.

"Hold on," Dereus said, then he launched us upward. He landed on the ledge then walked awhile. "We have a human guest area, but I'm not sure how well it has been maintained. It's been a while since a human was here. As they mentioned, the last time humans came, they started the human–dragon war, and that was well before your time. The area is still within this cave, so we don't have much farther to go."

We stayed quiet for the remainder of Dereus's trek down the different cave paths.

"We are here." Dereus knelt so we could get down.

I slid off into Gabe's waiting arms. "Thank you."

Gabe nodded and smiled at me. We both looked around at the small open area. I felt a little claustrophobic when I realized how deep within the mountain we must be. I saw no sign of light besides the dragon torches out in the main cave walkway. A single decaying bed stood by the back wall, but someone had put fresh leaves on it for padding.

"I'm sure you both could use some rest after your travels and the information you learned today. Rest tonight. You can talk about it all tomorrow. I will stay in the doorway here for the evening," Dereus said.

"You don't have to do that." I didn't want to keep him from wherever he was used to staying.

"I found you, so you are my responsibility until your future is decided."

"Are we in danger?" I hoped he would tell me no.

"Possibly. Not everyone is human friendly. They only post human-friendly dragons along the perimeter. A lot of dragons here have family who were murdered by humans during the war. Just the thought of peace disgusts them."

"Does that make you wonder if peace is even possible?" Gabe asked.

"It does, but enough of us want peace that we will be able to overrule the ones who want death for all humans. But for your peace of mind, I will be right here in the opening, and no dragon will get past me. You will be safe. So please, get some rest. You have a lot to talk about tomorrow."

"Thank you, Dereus. We appreciate all of your help," I said.

Dereus inclined his head then turned to wedge himself in the doorway.

My night was not filled with the sleep I needed but with nightmares of burning towns, murdered dragons, and death by fire. I didn't get enough rest to even begin thinking about world peace. Brenyx stayed close to my side and continued to watch me with an inclined head. Gabe snored away, and I was jealous of his deep sleep.

Brenyx and I moved to the other side of the small area so we wouldn't disturb Gabe.

"Brenyx, can you speak to me? I don't know how we are supposed to discuss this if you can't talk," I said.

Brenyx sat in front of me and inclined her head again.

"Am I supposed to consider all the options, talk them out,

and see how you respond? I mean, if we're going to save the world together, I'd like to at least hear your side."

Dereus stirred in the doorway, and I held my breath to see if he woke. Brenyx watched him too. Once his breathing steadied again, I looked back at Brenyx.

"Do you need to do your size-change thing? Come on. Give me something. You tried talking to me that one day but then stopped yourself. Why? What is the big deal if you speak to me? Or is it because we aren't bonded yet?" I gasped. "Because we were chosen together, if I decide yes or no, you have to go with it, and you don't actually have an opinion?"

Brenyx purred.

"I don't think that seems very fair. What if you don't like me?"

"It's obvious she does," Dereus said without turning around.

Tricky dragon. "I thought you were sleeping."

Dereus rolled onto his other side to face us. "Did you forget how you met me? I lie under a pile of rocks and don't move for hours on end. I am skilled in the ways of invisibility."

I laughed. "Well, I must say that you're quite good at it. I even thought you'd woken then gone back to sleep."

Dereus rumbled a chuckle. "Well, I did actually wake up then but could sense that you were having a conversation, so I didn't want to disturb you at first."

"At first?"

"Well, Brenyx may have tried speaking to you, but the law of the dragon stopped her. You are right that she cannot speak to you until you two have your ceremony. Speaking to each other is a form of bond between dragon and human."

"So only I will be able to speak to her? How can I hear you and all of the other dragons?" I asked.

"Oh no. Every human will be able to hear her either after

your ceremony or after the time for your ceremony has passed. This is to ensure that"—Dereus looked at Gabe, who stirred—"you humans, who are so easily influenced, cannot claim you were swayed by your bonded dragon."

"That makes no sense." I shook my head. "I could be just as easily influenced by you or any other dragon I spoke to. Even Chumana."

Dereus grinned. "No, child. You may hear all dragons, but we cannot influence you the same way a bonded dragon can. It's almost like magic, the amount of influence you have over each other. The reason for this is because normal humans would possibly die of terror as they ride their dragon and nose-dive and go through fire. So when you're bonded, you can remove each other's fear of both humans and dragons. You can understand things on a deeper level because you will be in each other's minds. It's not like having a conversation with someone else. You and Brenyx, if you choose to go through with the ceremony, will feel each other's feelings. If something makes you uncomfortable, she will know it the same moment you do. That's why the ceremony is a decision that you alone must make. Many humans are not strong enough or, sorry to say, smart enough to stand the bond with an ancient species."

Gabe stirred again, and I turned toward him. He sat up and looked at the three of us.

"Good morning," he mumbled and ran his hand through his hair.

"Good morning," Dereus and I said together.

I turned back to Dereus. "So how does one make a decision like this? I know it's been a long time, but how did the last bonded pair choose?"

Dereus slowly shook his head. "I cannot say. Once the human makes the decision, that is between the human and the dragon because the dragon will know. So you, Daughter of

Wisdom, need to consider this. Do you want to help solve the upset between the dragon and the human worlds? Or are you content to forget all about this and go back to the life you once had?"

"What do you mean forget all about this?" I asked.

Gabe settled beside me and grabbed my hand. I squeezed his, and he held on tight.

"We have a dragon that was not in the cavern who can make you both forget all about us. We don't want to start another war, so we have found the easiest way to prevent that is to make sure humans don't remember."

"So you're saying that's why we had so much trouble finding your exact location? You erase the memories of any humans who aren't a threat and send them back into human territory?" Gabe asked.

"Something close to that, yes." Dereus stood and stretched. "I am going to go find some food for us. You three should be safe in here. Dragons actively patrol these caves at this time of day, so nobody should bother you."

"And if they do bother us?" I asked.

Dereus grinned. "Well, we saw how Brenyx feels about someone bothering you, didn't we?"

I laughed and looked at Brenyx. She tucked her head behind her wing like a shy child. Dereus left us, and I sighed.

Gabe still held my hand and gave it another squeeze. "Don't overthink it, Sof. You just need to do what your heart tells you to."

If only it were that easy.

TWENTY-TWO

Gabe, Brenyx, and I were allowed to wander the entire cavern. Apparently, Baltasar had put a kill order out for any dragon that harmed us, as we were guests within their home. It seemed a little extreme, but I had to admit, I was grateful the moment I heard it. I felt a little less like I might die around any corner. Dereus, after feeding us a breakfast of some sort of roasted meat, left us alone for a while.

"What do you think you're going to do?" Gabe asked as we walked side by side.

Brenyx chirped and looked at me from my shoulder.

"I really don't know. I know you said to follow my heart, but my heart is a jumbled mess. I know what I should do, but I'm not sure I'm strong enough to do it."

Gabe took my hands in his, and we stopped walking.

"You are the Daughter of Wisdom, as everyone calls you. And they continue to call me the Son of Strength. What if we used my strength to help guide your wisdom?"

I searched his face for any sign of a joke but only found sincerity.

"You would give up your life to help me?"

"I wouldn't consider it giving up my life so much as joining yours."

I flushed and pulled my hands from his grasp. Brenyx purred and rubbed her cheek against mine.

"I didn't mean to offend—"

"No. No, you didn't offend me. It's just, I can't ask you to give up your life if this is what I choose, no matter how close of friends we've become," I said.

"Oh. I see. Friends, yeah." Gabe gave a tight-lipped smile and started walking down the cavern path.

I hurried to catch up to him. "I didn't mean to hurt you, Gabe."

Brenyx chittered and ran to my other shoulder then leaped onto Gabe's shoulder and nuzzled his cheek.

"Thanks, Brenyx." Gabe stopped walking and turned to me again. "You didn't hurt me. I just... Everything we've been through has been out of this world, and I just felt like we were maybe becoming closer."

"Oh... Oh." I startled. I had grown fond of Gabe, but I'd never seen myself marrying, and as a possible dragoness, that'd seemed even less likely.

"There you three are."

We all turned at Dereus's approach.

"I came to inform you that you will need to make your announcement at sundown. And just so you know, no matter which way you decide, your life will always be your own. Whether you choose to stay human or become a dragoness, it will always be you on the inside, deciding who you are."

I nodded. "Thank you, Dereus. I'm having a difficult time. I really wish Brenyx could talk to me because I don't think she'd sway me. I think she'd help me weigh the choice I'm about to make."

"It is not the way, but I understand."

"Have two people ever shared the bond with a single drag-on?" Gabe asked.

I looked at the floor and moved a small rock with my shoe. I knew Gabe wanted to help me, but I couldn't let him dedicate his life to me in that way. It wouldn't be fair, even if that was what he thought he wanted.

"Hmmm. I have never heard of such a thing, but that doesn't mean it isn't possible. Are you two considering sharing the duty?" Dereus asked.

"I guess you could say that," Gabe said.

"Well, I wouldn't be surprised, with the way you three already get along. Do you need anything before I go?" Dereus asked.

We shook our heads.

"No, I think we're all set. We'll just wander some more," I said.

"All right, then. I will find you again before it's time to make your announcement."

"Thank you, Dereus," Gabe said.

Dereus inclined his head then moseyed down the cavern path, his tail dragging behind him.

I turned and faced Gabe. "Gabe, you really don't need to do this. If I choose to go forward with this, it will take a lifetime. I can't ask you to dedicate your life like that."

Gabe smiled and tilted his head. "You didn't ask, so it's not like I'm being pressured. I just... I just want you to know that I'm here for you. That's all. No matter what you choose."

Brenyx nuzzled his cheek and purred.

"Thank you, Gabe."

We began walking again, following the direction Dereus

had taken. A shadow covered the cave wall, and I realized it was moving, growing larger as it came toward us.

Gabe swung his arm out in front of me. "Wait. I think that's a dragon. How are we supposed to know if it's nice or not?"

Brenyx chittered and leaped off Gabe's shoulder onto the ground. She took her stance in front of us, wings extended. I didn't laugh at her appearance anymore after I'd seen what she could grow to be.

The rumble of footsteps drew closer, and a dragon came around the corner ahead. It stopped short when it saw us.

"Kona?" I asked.

"Hey! You remember me! And they say humans can't remember anything. I mean, not me, of course. I don't say that. How are you?" Kona gave us a toothy grin and ambled up to tower over us.

"We're okay, I think," I said.

"Yeah, can't complain," Gabe said.

Brenyx had tucked her wings back to her sides, but she didn't come stand beside us just yet. She held herself tall, her spikes still up and ready, just in case.

"Are you nervous about the ceremony?" Kona asked.

Gabe and I looked at each other.

"A little. Is there a ceremony either way?" I asked.

"Sort of. A ceremony to bond you and Brenyx if you choose the life of a dragoness. Or a ceremony to wipe all dragon memories from your mind if you choose not to. Neither hurt. But all dragons are usually present. You'd better start heading toward the cavern, though. Sundown is not far away, and for two humans walking, it'll take a little longer to get there. No offense," Kona said.

I giggled. "None taken, Kona. It was good to see you."

"It was good to see you three as well. I never thought I'd live to meet the next possible dragoness."

We moved out of the way and stood closer to the cave wall so Kona could continue on his way.

"Do you have any idea which way the cavern is?" Gabe asked.

I laughed. "Um. No, actually. Maybe we should've asked Kona."

Brenyx snapped her teeth at us.

"What?" Gabe and I asked together.

Brenyx shook her head and started forward.

"Well, I guess Brenyx knows which way it is," I said.

And the three of us walked toward what would be the rest of our lives.

I was surprised that Brenyx knew exactly which direction the cavern was in. She did not miss a single turn, and we wound up in the exact same place where we'd arrived with Dereus the day before. I stood a couple of feet away from the ledge and took in the cavern once more, staring at the platform where I would have to make a decision that would affect the rest of my life. And Brenyx's too. *Would she remember me if I chose to return to the human world?*

Gabe stepped up beside me and put his arm around my shoulders. "No matter what you choose, I'll be there for you."

I teared up. Just a few weeks ago, I had tried to get him out of my life as another stupid suitor. And he was ready to devote his life to me and the cause.

"Thank you, Gabe. I appreciate that more than you'll ever know."

I put my hand on top of his, and we put our heads together as we stood staring at the cavern. I imagined it full of dragons. If I chose to be a dragoness, then some of those dragons would hate me, but they already did. The whole point was to help bring peace between dragons and humans. *Could I do that? If I had Gabe, could we do that?* The dragons said I would never belong to dragons or humans again. *What would Chumana want me to do?* She had faith that I could take care of Brenyx. She had faith that everything would be okay. The dragons had said it was no accident that she and I had met.

Brenyx wound herself around my ankles then sat next to my foot with her tail wrapped around my leg. I smiled, imagining she did that to make sure I didn't try to get away from her. I wondered what she would sound like. *Would she sound like her mother or have her own distinct voice?* She looked up at me and tilted her head.

"You can't hear my mind already, can you?"

Brenyx chittered and shook her head.

"Okay. Just making sure."

"Why? You have thoughts you don't want anybody else to hear?" Gabe asked.

I grinned. "No, of course not. I'm a lady."

We stared at each other for about five seconds before we burst into laughter.

"Ahem."

We turned, and Dereus stood not far behind us. I was surprised I hadn't felt him walking up to us because the ground shook with every step he took.

"Hi, Dereus." I cleared my throat. "Is it time already?"

"Just about. Have you made your decision?"

Gabe and Brenyx both raised their brows, seemingly hopeful that my answer would be yes.

"No. I think I'll know when it's officially time to decide. I mean, I am leaning one way more than the other, but I haven't had a solid yes or no pop into my mind yet."

"I didn't think this was a pop-into-your-mind kind of decision," Dereus said.

"Oh. No. Not like that. I mean... I guess... Well, I have no idea what I mean."

"Mm-hmm." Dereus nodded. "I know what you mean. You've had less than a day to decide your entire future. Most humans don't make decisions like that. Humans can change their minds. What you're doing is deciding the rest of your life. But you will have to decide one way or another. Dragons are not known for their patience."

I nodded. Gabe took my hand.

"You'll know when you know," Gabe said.

I squeezed his hand. "Yes, I think I will."

A gust of wind pushed me, and I turned to see dragons arriving. My chest tightened, and I thought I might vomit. The time to officially decide was there.

"We will wait until the cavern is mostly full, then I'll fly you down," Dereus said.

I still held Gabe's hand. "Can Gabe come with us?"

"I, well, I don't know. I suppose I can take him down with you. The platform is big enough that he can stand off to the side. And if he's not allowed, I'm sure I'll be instructed to take him with me. I won't be too far from you. And don't forget, you will be safe."

"Okay," I whispered. Any courage I'd thought I had was slipping away with each passing second.

We waited for several minutes. It didn't take as long as I'd hoped for the cavern to fill.

"We should go down now," Dereus said.

I could tell by his whisper that he was trying to be gentle with a fragile human but not condescending. All the dragons who hoped that I would save them were there. Others hated me and didn't even know me but knew that humans had killed their families. *Is peace even possible?*

TWENTY-THREE

Dereus carefully deposited us onto the platform before the council arrived. Gabe stood about twenty feet from me. I didn't want him too far from me for two reasons. One, he comforted me. And two, I feared that if he stood too close to the ledge, it would be easy for a dragon to create a gust of wind and knock him down into the dark abyss that surrounded the platform. Gabe gave me a single encouraging nod. I returned it then faced forward to wait for the council.

Brenyx sat on my shoulder, and she, too, waited for the council's arrival. I looked at her out of the corner of my eye, and she turned to face me.

"Brrp?"

"Oh, nothing. I just wanted to look at you one last time before our lives were changed forever. I'll either be with you the rest of my life, or I'll not remember the time I've spent with you since the day I met your mother."

Brenyx nodded and returned her attention to the council seating area. About one minute later, Baltasar, Sule, and Galik emerged onto the platform. I gasped when I saw Fennewick with them. Now that I wasn't terrified of him, I was mesmerized by his beauty. His blue scales sparkled as he moved, almost as if he were made of crystal. He gazed down at us, and my breath caught. My anxiety crept back up, but I refused to rub my chest and reveal my feelings in front of all those dragons, Fennewick most of all. He wanted to kill me, yet there he sat with the council members. But he only wanted to kill me because he thought I'd killed Chumana. I didn't know why he hadn't come to meet Brenyx yet.

"Silence!" Baltasar yelled, and everyone immediately fell quiet.

I swallowed my anxiety and took a deep breath. Brenyx wrapped her tail around my neck just a little tighter. I wanted to thank her, but I was sure as my body relaxed a little that she knew.

"Now, we are all here for this rare occasion. Brenyx and Sofia may become one." Baltasar held my eyes with his own. "But only Sofia is allowed to make the decision. If she so chooses, she will be bound to Brenyx for life. Their bond will bring peace to humans and dragons so we may coexist as we once did, many ages ago. If Sofia chooses to return to her human life, she will not remember that she had this adventure with dragons. She will not even have an inkling that dragons exist. Daughter of Wisdom, do you understand these terms?"

I cleared my throat and shouted, "Yes!" I did not want to appear weak in front of the dragons.

"Sofia, what is your decision?"

Really? That fast? No fancy anything? I looked at Brenyx, and she gave me a single, sharp nod. I looked at Gabe, and he did the same thing.

"I—" I cleared my throat again. "I choose to accept my

bond to Brenyx and bring peace between humans and dragons."

Brenyx trilled, but her sound was drowned out by dragon roars. They flapped their wings, and some even blew fire. Brenyx circled my neck and rubbed her cheek against mine as if pleased with my answer. Gabe beamed and gave me a thumbs-up then clapped. Baltasar surveyed the dragons, watching over the cavern. I couldn't help but wonder if he had taken note of the dragons who had left. I was grateful to see it was probably less than twenty of them. That meant the majority of dragons supported the plan. Fennewick had remained remarkably still. *Does it anger him that his daughter is about to be bonded to a human?* Maybe he was angry that Chumana left with his egg. Maybe she was looking for the dragoness. Unless he spoke to me, I would never know.

Baltasar continued to watch the dragons. When they finally quieted down, he said, "Thank you all who stayed. We will now begin the ceremony. Fennewick, if you're ready."

Fennewick? What does he have to do with this?

He spread his wings without disrupting the council and glided down to the platform. I worried his air would knock Gabe right over the edge, but Gabe took a few steps forward so he was safe. Fennewick landed gracefully, folded his wings, and approached us. He glanced once at Gabe but otherwise didn't acknowledge his presence. He stopped about ten feet in front of us, and I craned my neck to look up at him.

"Sofia, Daughter of Wisdom, and Brenyx, Daughter of Chumana, do you solemnly swear to protect both humans and dragons, to bring peace to our kinds for so long as you both shall live?"

"I do," I said as Brenyx chirped and nodded.

"And will you both protect your kind even if it surely means your own death?"

"I do."

Brenyx chirped again.

"Do you promise to stay true to each other and never sacrifice your bond for anyone or anything?"

"I do."

Brenyx chirped.

"Now, are you both ready?" Fennewick took a couple of steps backward.

I looked at Brenyx, and we nodded.

"Then let's begin the ceremony."

Fennewick's blue scales brightened until a white glow surrounded his entire body. He inhaled through his mouth and blew a white fire straight at us. I cringed and closed my eyes. Brenyx pushed her face into my neck. Despite thinking I would die in that moment, the fire was cold. When the sensation stopped, I opened my eyes and saw that we were surrounded by ice, almost like we stood on a frozen pond.

I risked a glance at Gabe. He stood completely still, his eyes wide and mouth open. He must've thought we would die by fire too. My body warmed, and it had nothing to do with what Fennewick had just done. I felt that Gabe was connected to Brenyx and me. I looked at her, and she looked at me then Gabe then back at me. She nodded so hard I thought her head might pop off. Fennewick stared at us but did not move. *Did he know I would try this?* I made eye contact with Gabe and extended my hand in invitation.

Gabe's eyebrows drew together like he was confused, so I beckoned him. I checked Fennewick, and he still stood waiting. I wiggled my fingers at Gabe again, and Brenyx swished her tail impatiently. Gabe blinked a few times then hurried to the edge of our pond. He looked at Fennewick, and if a dragon could smile, Fennewick did.

"I wondered if you girls would be smart enough to realize

that you have a rare companion. Son of Strength, do you promise to uphold all of the requirements of the bond?"

"I do." Gabe held his head high.

"Then please join Brenyx and Sofia." Fennewick gestured for Gabe to stand by us.

Gabe cautiously stepped onto the ice. I wasn't sure what any of us expected. Brenyx trilled and pranced on my shoulder. Gabe reached out and took my hand, and Brenyx ran across my shoulders then our arms to his shoulder. She rubbed her cheek against his then went down his arm and settled on our hands, her tail wrapping around my wrist. I smiled at her. We had been like a little family since she'd been born, and now we would be a family forever.

"This will not hurt, but you will feel a strong sensation under your skin. Do not be afraid," Fennewick said.

Gabe squeezed my hand, so I squeezed his back. No matter what Fennewick said, I was afraid. I waited for the sensation to hit me and watched Fennewick for any sign of its arrival. He again inhaled as if to blow fire on us, and my heart lurched at the sight of flame in his throat. I squeezed my eyes shut as fire flew toward us. I braced for the burn, but he had been right. It wasn't pain. My body felt hot, like when I got into the bathtub too quickly after putting boiling water into it. Thankfully, the sensation was over almost as quickly as it began.

I opened my eyes. Brenyx's eyes were wide, and Gabe's face stayed scrunched. I squeezed his hand, and he blinked a few times, his nose still wrinkled. We made eye contact, and his hand relaxed.

"Your eyes," Gabe said.

I instinctively touched my face but didn't feel anything bad. Then I noticed Gabe's eyes.

"Your eyes... they look... look like a dragon's!"

"Yours do too!"

Fennewick chuckled and shook his head. "You three now have a bond that will last for the rest of your lifetime. You carry the burden of bringing peace to this world. You no longer fully belong to the human world nor the dragon world, but you will always have each other. Thank you for devoting your lives to benefit the rest of us. Now, as you adjust to your new selves, you will need time to rest. We've made up a room for you to share. Enjoy this rest tonight, as your journey begins tomorrow."

TWENTY-FOUR

The next day, I felt rushed. Rushed to eat. Rushed to wash my face. Rushed to see the council. Dereus ambled along in front of us like I was in trouble and on my way to the principal. Gabe held my hand, and Brenyx rode on my shoulder. Every now and then, Gabe squeezed my palm. His eyes met mine, and he gave me a reassuring smile. I couldn't help but feel anxious. Sure, we were the new trio to save the dragons, but I couldn't help but look over my shoulder to see if a murderous dragon was after us. Though I was pretty sure I would've felt their footsteps. Dereus's steps vibrated through my feet.

Dereus stopped before a doorway and turned toward us. "The council is waiting for you in there. But don't worry. They are fully supportive of you. Three is an unusual group, but we could all tell you had a special bond when you arrived. Almost as if you were already mates."

I choked on my spit and cleared my throat. I wasn't sure if it was my or Gabe's hand, but soon, our palms were sweaty, so I pulled my hand out of his and wiped it on my pants.

Dereus turned his head to look at us. "I didn't mean it as a bad thing. You humans are so sensitive. I can feel your skin heat up from here."

Oh, great. That made it even worse. That time, Gabe cleared his throat. Brenyx chittered and rubbed my face. I giggled and shooed her away. She chittered again. She hadn't begun talking to us yet. I wasn't sure if she couldn't or if she didn't want to, but I was grateful that she wasn't speaking just yet so she couldn't embarrass me further.

"We're here." Dereus stopped on the opposite side of a doorway.

"Aren't you coming in with us?" I asked.

"No. This is between you and the council now. They will give you greater details of what is expected of you and what you can expect. I will be in my den. Please be sure that you stop to say goodbye before you leave."

"You won't be staying?" Gabe asked.

Dereus shook his head. "You'll learn more now. Go along. And please come see me."

"We will," Gabe and I said together.

Dereus nodded and went back the way we had come. I hoped someone would guide us to his den because I wasn't entirely certain where it was. Maybe Brenyx would.

"It is impolite to linger in the doorway," someone called.

Gabe and I hurried into the room, Brenyx holding tightly to my neck with her tail.

"Our apologies. We didn't mean to delay," I said.

"We are not angry, Daughter of Wisdom. Please, come forward," Baltasar said.

We hurried toward the council. Fennewick was also present. He stood to the side and looked much happier to see us, grinning as we entered. Perhaps he was warming to us since we would be leaving.

"Thank you for seeing us." Sule smiled. "We are so pleased that you made the decision to help both of our kinds. It has been many years since we have seen peace. I would very much like to see it again in my lifetime. But that is not to say this will be an easy journey for you."

"You will be forced to make some difficult decisions, more difficult than you would have thought to face in your previous life. But with the combined power between the three of you, none of us has a single doubt you will succeed," Galik said.

"And you will always have us four to count on when you need anything, whether it be help or if you need us to show humans that we can be peaceful. Or if you just need a break, because this will be an exhausting journey," Baltasar said.

"I am so proud that you made this decision. And I am even prouder that the one selected was my own daughter. You look so much like your mother. And now, I am thrilled to give you your voice. Are you ready?" Fennewick asked.

Brenyx nodded so hard I had to catch her as she fell off my shoulder. I set her down, and she stepped toward Fennewick. She stood, spikes, head, and tail high. She was adorable. I wondered what she would be like fully grown—if she would keep her silly personality or if she would grow to be more serious like her father.

Gabe and I stepped back, giving Brenyx and Fennewick room. Brenyx's tail swished a little slower than it had before. She must've been a little nervous.

"This is a lot less complicated than your ceremony." Fennewick crouched and put his head on the ground in front of Brenyx. He took a deep breath then blew air on her face.

I had expected fire or a glow or something visible. It was very anticlimactic. After the single breath, Fennewick sat up.

"Brenyx, you now have your voice. Use it well," Fennewick said.

Brenyx did a happy jump in a circle. She stopped when she faced Gabe and me. "It's so nice to finally speak to you."

I smiled. She didn't sound like Chumana at all. She sounded like a little girl.

"It's so nice to hear your voice and be able to better communicate with you," I said.

"You did pretty well even without my voice, though." Brenyx tilted her head with a grin.

"Now that you three are complete, we have one more gift before you can leave. You can't possibly have expected us to send you on your way without any knowledge. So we have what we like to call an expert in both dragons and humans," Fennewick said.

Baltasar gave a single, small roar, which I took as a summons. A beautiful red dragon with matching fire-red eyes came into the room from a side entrance.

"This, here, is Bokruz. He is our resident human expert. He will accompany you on your journey for as long as you need," Baltasar said.

"Thank you, Baltasar, for that introduction." Bokruz inclined his head toward the council. He turned his attention back to us. "But you can call me Bo. It's exciting to finally get out into the field again."

"We are pleased to have you, Bo," Gabe said.

"Yes, we are happy to have you," I said.

Brenyx nodded between us. I wondered if she'd forgotten that she had a voice after not having one for so long.

"We will leave you to your plans. We wish you all luck, and please know that we support you in all you do. If you ever need anything, please just return here, and we will meet with you to see how we can help," Baltasar said.

"Good luck," Sule and Galik said together.

All three council members inclined their heads. Gabe,

Brenyx, and I did the same. Fennewick lingered but didn't say more, so he must plan to stay, at least for a while. I supposed, since he was the king, he could do anything he wanted.

"You must have so many questions about dragons. I probably have just as many about humans. You really are an interesting species. I've studied humans for years but have not interacted with any. No one wanted me to be the reason the next war started. I've waited a long time for this." Bo rocked from foot to foot.

"I didn't even know dragons were still around until Chumana came into my life." I grinned at Brenyx. "But it's the best thing that ever happened to me."

"How about we go over what we know, then we can lay out a plan of sorts?" Bo said.

"Well, if it's okay with you, I'd really like to go check on my brother. He took an arrow to the leg from a dragon hunter on our way here. He was supposed to go back to Carstel, but I'm not sure if he continued on home. We figured our mother would become frantic with us gone for so long. He was supposed to be my chaperone," I said.

Fennewick and Bo grinned at me.

"We do admire the familial traits of humans being so close. Dragons don't always stay close to their parents or children. Sometimes, but not often," Bo said.

That explained why Fennewick hadn't rushed to meet Brenyx.

"Now, let's go over some plans," Fennewick said.

CHAPTER
TWENTY-FIVE

After a teary—on my part—goodbye with Fennewick then Dereus, our little save-the-world team made up of two dragons and two humans walked to the edge of the caves. We stood on the same ledge that Dereus had first brought us to. I turned and looked back into the cave, and sadness filled me. I only hoped I could be as strong as they thought I was. I wished that we could stay longer and learn more about dragons, but Bo and Fennewick both insisted urgency was key. A war hadn't been waged in a long time, and they feared one was on its way. Especially with how we had been attacked by Bella's father. That meant dragon hunters were just waiting for the perfect opportunity to get their hands on dragons.

"I think it's best if you all ride on my back. We can head down the trail you took to get here. But I will land well before we get close to the town. We can walk the rest of the way. Or you could still ride on my back, and I will walk," Bo said.

"Sounds good to me. You ready, Sof and Brenyx?" Gabe asked.

I shrugged. "Ready as I'll ever be. I'm excited to see Oliver, though. I hope that his leg has started to heal."

"You'll be okay, Sofia. Starting is always the hardest part. Once you have your first experience as peacemaker, you will better understand what to do. And don't worry, we will come back here. You're looking at the cave as if it's the last time you will ever see it," Bo said.

"He's right. We'll all be okay." Brenyx, who still enjoyed riding on my shoulder, rubbed her cheek against mine.

"I know we will. It's just, a lot has happened really fast. I'm just taking it all in. We should go, though. I can't wait to see my brother. We haven't been apart for longer than a day since I was born. And I'm sure he's wondering if we're still alive. Him getting shot on our first day of the trip wasn't exactly a good omen," I said.

Nobody spoke, but we all nodded. We hoped it would be a successful trip. I knew tough times loomed ahead. It wouldn't be life without them, but we just hoped for more good than bad.

"Okay, let's go. Time to see Oliver," I said.

Bo inclined his head and knelt so we could climb onto his back. Gabe gestured for me to go first, so I climbed up and grabbed onto one of Bo's spikes. Gabe leaped up behind me and wrapped his arms around my waist.

"We're ready, Bo, whenever you are," I said.

Bo nodded, stood, and stretched his wings. "Okay, then. Here we go."

With a blast of air that about pulled his spike from my hands, we were off. Bo plunged, leveled out, then flapped us up toward the mountains where we had met Dereus. Once Bo was mostly gliding with an occasional flap of his wings, I released my death grip on his spike and looked around. The mountain area was beautiful. The lower hills looked a bit like broccoli with the trees so tightly packed. The higher up the mountain, the fewer trees grew.

We passed over the mountain peak where we'd arrived. Then I was surprised that instead of going straight, Bo flew to the path that went along the base of the mountains. It seemed like such a long way, but as fast as Bo flew, we quickly reached the road that led to Gabe's house in Carstel and Oliver. I watched for our horses. I wasn't sure if they would be smart enough to return to Gabe's or if they would continue along until they found food and water.

What had taken us days by horse would maybe take a day before we reached town with how fast the ground zoomed by. I watched along the path, squinting as we traveled. Something was on the trail.

"Bo!" I hollered. "What is that?"

Bo looked down and froze in midair. His entire body went invisible. I could see right through him, as if Gabe, Brenyx, and I sat on air, floating in the sky. If anyone looked up, that was what they would see. Bo circled until we were out of sight of whoever was below us. I could feel his head moving left to right and back again as he looked around. Soon, I spotted what he was searching for. A small clearing. We descended, and Bo knelt so Gabe and I could quickly dismount.

"Can you turn back? Not being able to see you freaks me out," Gabe said.

"Sorry." Bo changed back to the beautiful red dragon he was. "I don't know how well humans can see, but could you tell that those were hunters?"

"Excuse me?"

"Hunters. They had bows, swords, and any other pointy object that they could find. There had to be at least twenty of them. I think they're heading to the north mountains to try and kill the dragons." Bo's voice rose higher with each word. His eyes darted around, not focusing on anything.

"Bo. Bo." I raised my hands to touch him, trying to get him to look down at me.

He finally calmed enough to stop moving, and he looked directly into my eyes.

"We are the peacekeepers. Let's try to keep the peace. Don't panic. You can remain invisible. I will go and talk to them—"

"We will go and talk to them," Gabe cut in.

I smiled at him. "Yes, we, us three, will go and talk to them. Perhaps we can reason with them."

"Or they could be angry that you killed their friend and got away with a dragon egg worth a lot of money. You could get killed on your very first outing just miles away from the north mountains. Do you really want to risk it?" Bo asked.

"Bo, if we don't risk it, those people could go straight to the mountains, discover the dragons, and start the next war. Let me try to reason with them. If we can't stop an angry horde of twenty or so people, how are we supposed to stop the next dragon–human war?" I asked.

Bo considered that for a moment. He tilted his head and looked between Gabe, Brenyx, and me.

"I suppose we should. I mean, it's what we are here for. Or going around for. Do you have a plan? They seemed pretty angry," Bo said.

"What if we just try to talk to them?" Gabe asked.

"I'm not so sure that's a wise idea," Bo said.

"Why not?" I asked.

"Have you looked at your eyes lately? You have dragon eyes. I don't think this dragon-hungry horde is going to be willing to talk to you. And what if they recognize you? You were recently in town. Plus, if they're ready to kill, they'll strike you down," Bo said.

"Well, what if I stay back far enough at first so they can't tell? Do you think that would work?" I asked.

"It'll have to be enough," Gabe said.

We all agreed, then we mounted Bo to prepare for our first mission.

Bo landed in the closest clearing he could find next to the group of men. "I will be invisible above you. We should have a signal if you need my help."

"I'm pretty sure that if they start attacking us, that will be a good signal." Gabe slid off of Bo.

I wanted to laugh but knew that it was such a real possibility, I couldn't. Or maybe shouldn't. I slid off of Bo next.

"Good point," Bo said.

"I thought so," Gabe said.

"Okay. Let's see if we can reason with this horde. Brenyx, are you ready?" I asked.

"Ready." Brenyx gave a single determined nod.

"Well, then, I guess, here we go." I led the way into the woods.

TWENTY-SIX

It didn't take long to find the men. They clanged their swords on their shields and shouted as if they wanted to announce their arrival. Gabe and I walked up the road to where we could face them from a little ways away. I hoped they wouldn't be able to see our eyes.

"Brenyx, I think you should stay hidden just until we learn their intentions. They may only be after you, and in that case, I definitely don't want you where they can take you," I said.

"They can try, but they won't succeed." Brenyx's spikes stood straight in the air.

"I know they won't, but I just want to try to deescalate this as quickly as possible. To be completely honest, I'm scared. I don't actually know what we're doing. I wish for so many things, but one of them is more time, which I know we don't have."

"Let's go," Gabe said.

Brenyx ran down my arm and leaped onto the ground. She walked between Gabe and me, her tail swishing.

We reached the road, and I couldn't quite see the men yet. I reached out and took Gabe's hand. He squeezed mine and smiled half-heartedly. I let go, and we approached the oncoming horde. Brenyx walked into the woods and followed alongside us.

We stopped just as they came into sight around the bend. It took about thirty seconds or so before anybody even noticed we were there.

A burly man with a thick black mustache and beard held out his arms like a bird in flight. Everyone eventually paid enough attention to realize he was stopping them.

"What are two young pups like you doing all the way out here?" the man asked, glaring at us.

"We were wondering the same about you," I said.

"I don't go about telling my business to strangers," the man said.

"Well, neither do I," I said.

"You seem awfully brave or stupid for just the two of you to confront us." He looked behind him and laughed, and the rest of the men laughed too. He was obviously their ringleader. "And all the way out here. Only one thing could possibly bring you here. Are you two dragon sympathizers?"

Gabe and I glanced at each other. We weren't expecting that.

"And if we are?" Gabe asked.

"Then you'd better move aside and let us pass," the man said as a few chuckled behind him. He sneered, revealing some nasty yellow-and-black teeth.

"I'm afraid we just can't do that. We cannot allow you to harm the dragons. We won't allow another war, and if you try to harm them, that's exactly what will happen." My heart thundered inside my chest like I was on the verge of a panic attack. I held my breath to slow my heart.

"And how exactly do you plan on stopping us?"

"My charm, of course. Now, please turn back and stop this madness. You cannot possibly think you could defeat dragons. Please, learn about them. Understand them. Just don't hurt them," I pleaded.

The burly man wrinkled his forehead. "Enough. Get them!" he yelled as he waved his arm forward.

"No!" I flung my hands out in front of me and squeezed my eyes shut.

Screams, panicked screams, filled my ears. I opened my eyes and saw a wall of fire blasting from my hands, stopping the horde. Gabe gaped at me, his eyes wide and his mouth open. Brenyx had appeared by my other side, a look of satisfaction on her face.

"How do I stop it?" I cried.

Nowhere to be seen, Bo said, "Make a fist."

I squeezed my hands into fists, and the flame extinguished. No fire remained. It was as if I put out the flame just by covering my palms.

"Witchcraft!" one of the men yelled.

"A dragon!" another called.

"Please! We don't want a war. Just stop. There has to be a way," I said.

The horde stood like a group of chastised schoolchildren caught putting a lizard in their teacher's cup. Even the burly man opened his mouth like a fish out of water as if he couldn't quite think of whether to stay or run. The rest of his horde looked between him and our little group. I checked behind me and was glad that Bo had chosen to stay hidden.

"Let's get out of here," someone said, and slowly, several backed away with him.

About three-quarters of the group turned and ran the way they had come.

The burly man yelled, "Cowards!" after them.

Only five men remained.

"You just wait until we see you again, witch. This isn't over. You best be watching for your precious dragons. When we come back, there'll be more of us. Mark my words." The burly man stood straight, took a few steps backward, then turned and hurried away.

Once they were out of sight, Gabe turned to me. "That was amazing! Did you know we could do that? How—"

I fell into darkness.

CHAPTER

TWENTY-SEVEN

I woke with Bo's face so close to mine that he was all that I could see. I groaned. My head throbbed, and my stomach lurched. I rolled onto my side in case I threw up only to realize that my head was in Gabe's lap. Bo backed up enough that I could look around. We were still in the center of the road.

"What happened?" I tried to prop my cheek on Gabe's knee. I didn't want to throw up all over him if that was what came next.

"Well, I was asking if you knew that we could do that, then you blacked out." Gabe petted my hair.

"I caught you," Bo said.

I grinned. "Thanks, guys. How long was I out?"

"It's only been about a half hour. You didn't use that much energy since it was such a short time," Bo said.

"So, this is a normal thing now that we're bound with Brenyx?" I asked.

"Yes, it is. You three will discover that you have more power together. That heat you felt during the ceremony was the fire being placed in your veins. The only thing is, not everyone can use it or call it at their will. It's the law of nature that will determine if you are worthy of it in that moment. Once, a long time ago, a human received the power of flame and became so power hungry that he lost sight of the cause. He wound up terrorizing people to get whatever he wanted. We historians believe that is why it will show up for some and not others, and you can only summon it for good. If any ill will lies in your heart, the flame will not come to you. And if you use it for good and don't want to pass out, the flame will need to pass between you three. Well, I'm guessing there. Never have two humans been involved in a single connection before. So, as you three are a little odd and have never been written about in history, we will have to learn some things as we go," Bo said.

"Well, I'm ready to make those history books." Gabe laughed.

I smiled, but I wasn't so sure I was ready to make history. I still felt woozy. "I think I'll start my history making just trying to sit up."

"Take it slow." Gabe helped me into a sitting position, and Brenyx plopped herself in front of me.

I held my head in my hands, waiting for the trees to stop spinning. "If this is what it'll be like every time we use the flame, I don't want it."

Bo laughed. "Oh, Sofia, you have much to learn. It will only do this to you the first few times, until your body adjusts. And like I said, if you three share it between you, it won't drain you. Or it shouldn't. I don't want to make any definitive comments until we learn how everything works."

"Do you think you can fly, Sofia? Or would it be better to stay on the ground?" Brenyx asked.

"I think if you and Gabe hold onto me, we should be able to

fly. I want to get back to Oliver and make sure he's okay. Then, maybe we can rest awhile," I said.

My companions nodded at me. I was sure they wouldn't mind a little bit of rest as well. Bo knelt, and Gabe and Brenyx helped me onto his back. I held on tight to a spike on Bo's neck, and Gabe wrapped his arms around me. Brenyx positioned herself in front of me between the next spike, and she wrapped her tail around my wrist.

"Hang on." Bo launched himself straight up into the air with a burst from his wings. He turned himself invisible shortly after launching.

I felt Gabe lean over and look down, probably looking for the horde, just like I was. *Who knew if they seriously were scared enough to leave? But would they come back with a bigger group like the man had threatened?* I was supposed to be making things better, not increasing the chances of a larger attack. But before I worried about that and the future of mankind, I just needed to know Oliver was okay.

It was amazing how much faster one could travel by dragon than by horse, because it didn't feel very long before Gabe said, "Bo, you need to turn east just a little. My house isn't much farther."

Bo leaned to the left then leveled out, heading straight for Gabe's house. When it came into view, relief filled half of me, but the other half wouldn't be full until we saw Oliver.

"Just land in the back courtyard, Bo," Gabe said.

Bo began his descent. I looked around to see if anybody had noticed two humans floating through the air. But I didn't see anybody. I never spotted a single one of the horde, either. I wondered if they had taken to the trees to avoid being seen. Bo sank lower and landed gracefully on the grass. His feet had barely touched before I slid down his side.

"Oliver!" I called and stumbled toward the house. "Oliver!"

Gabe caught up to me and held my elbow. Brenyx scampered along by my other side. She obviously didn't care if anybody saw her. I kept my eyes on the door, willing Oliver to come outside and greet us. We were almost to the door when Harold opened it.

"Gabriel? Sofia? Are you all right?" Harold rushed down the steps to my side, nearly stepping on Brenyx. She jumped out of the way and continued beside us.

"We're okay. Is Oliver here?" I asked as they helped me up the steps.

"He is. Come inside. I will take you to him," Harold said.

I looked all around for Oliver and saw him nowhere. I wanted to call out, but Harold was taking me to him. He led us to the parlor, and I saw my brother sitting, facing us.

"Oliver!" I broke free from Harold and Gabe and rushed to him. Crying, I hugged him as tightly as I could.

"Oh, Sofia. I'm so glad you're okay." Oliver squeezed me back. "I've been so worried about you. And, uh, so have Mother and Father."

I pulled back from him, held his shoulders, and searched his face.

"Your eyes... but, um." Oliver looked over my shoulder.

I turned to see what he was looking at, and there sat both my parents.

"Mother? Father?" I almost couldn't believe they were there. "What are you doing here?"

"Well, when your two children go missing, despite what the letters say, your parents come looking," Mother said.

Father rose from his chair and embraced me, clutching me tight to his chest. "We were so worried about you. And your brother came clean and told us what journey you were on. And that fancy egg we thought was to be your dowry."

"Are you angry with me?" I asked into Father's chest. I wasn't ready to let go of him yet.

"Never. We're just glad you're okay." Father held me close.

Mother, I noticed, did not come hug me. She was likely thinking of all the unladylike things I'd done. Plus, wearing pants was probably not the best way to greet her. And I must've smelled and looked a mess after not bathing for so long.

"Mr. and Mrs. Taylor, it's a pleasure to see you both." Gabe came into my line of sight.

Father released me and looked at him. I wasn't sure which way things would play out. *Would he be furious about the lies?*

Instead, Father surprised us all and stuck out his hand. "Gabriel. Thank you for keeping my daughter safe."

Gabe sighed in relief as he shook Father's hand. "Well, I had help. Oliver was amazing, and we had a couple more friends as well."

Father tilted his head, then Brenyx came into view from behind the chair.

"You have lovely children, Mr. and Mrs. Taylor. You raised them well," Brenyx said.

Father gaped at her. Mother looked green.

"Um. Thank you?" Father finally looked into my eyes, and his mouth fell open.

"Yes, we have a lot to talk about. But first, I'd like to introduce you to another new friend. He's outside. Oliver, can you join us?" I looked at my brother and the crutch that lay beside him.

"Yes," Oliver said, and our little group, including Mother, went outside.

"Bo, you can show yourself," Gabe called.

Bo shimmered like crystal until he turned his normal brilliant red. Harold caught Mother as she fainted. Oliver whooped, and Father turned to face me.

"I always knew you were meant for more than fancy dresses," Father said.

WE ALL SAT OUTSIDE to include Bo in the conversation. He was a little too large to fit in the doorway of the house, and we didn't want to leave him by himself while the rest of us caught up.

After we had filled everybody in about our journey, I asked, "Does anybody have questions?"

"Will your eyes always look like that?" Mother asked, her voice trembling.

"Yes, they will," Bo answered for me. "She is our official dragoness and is a key component in stopping the next dragon–human war. The bond that she explained will be forever. She will make history, your daughter."

I smiled gratefully at him because, despite it all, Mother still seemed to think that I would go home and marry.

"Mother, I'm very happy. You still have Oliver to stay and marry well. But we need to stop the war before it starts. Perhaps, when I'm done, marriage will be a thought, but for now, I cannot return home. Nobody will accept me with the way I look. I was warned that I will never be part of the dragon or the human world. I am somewhere in between."

Father grinned at me and took Mother's hand. "Don't worry about her eyes, dear. Didn't you hear any of the story? Gabriel has the same eyes as Sofia, and they are forever bonded to Brenyx. It may not be the traditional wedding you were looking for, but Sofia is now bonded to one of the greatest families for the rest of her life."

Mother's face softened as she surveyed Gabe and his huge

spare home. She managed a weak smile. Progress. Gabe winked at me. I flushed and cleared my throat.

"I love all of you. I do. But for now, I cannot return home. We have been given an incredible task that I intend to see through. And after meeting some of my best new friends, Gabe, Brenyx, Bo, and I need to continue to fight for dragons everywhere," I said.

"Yes. Until we can get humans and dragons to understand and trust each other, we can't just sit around and do nothing. We must help them," Gabe said.

Father stood and stepped in front of me. I stood too.

"I am so proud of you, Sofia. I know you can do this. And I know Chumana would be so proud of you too." Father pulled me into what seemed like his hundredth hug since I'd returned. For a man of so few words, his statement filled me with enough courage that I knew our little group could make a difference in the world.

"Thank you, Father. We won't let you down."

I looked over my little, oddly formed family and felt proud of them. Despite all our differences, we were about to save the dragon–human world.

Thank you for taking the time to read this book.

Sylviane Stoltzman lives in Minnesota with her husband and six cats. She loves cats as much as books. You can find her nonfiction writing about cats at www.thecatlick.com. When she isn't writing, she is sure to be reading, watching movies, racing go-karts, or spending time with family.

facebook.com/sylvianestoltzmanauthor

www.ingramcontent.com/pod-product-compliance
Lightning Source LLC
Chambersburg PA
CBHW020113310726

48970CB00002B/616